The Two Wealthy Farmers

By Hannah More

Grace & Truth Books
Sand Springs, Oklahoma

ISBN # 1-58339-128-2

Originally Published by The American Tract Society
  of New York
Printed by Triangle Press, 1996
Current printing, Grace & Truth Books, 2004

Cover design by Ben Gundersen

Grace & Truth Books
3406 Summit Boulevard
Sand Springs, Oklahoma   74063
Phone: 918 245 1500

www.graceandtruthbooks.com
email: gtbooksorders@cs.com

TABLE OF CONTENTS

THE TWO WEALTHY FARMERS

Part 1

THE VISIT

Mr. Bragwell and Mr. Worthy happened to meet last year at Weyhill Fair. They were glad to see each other, as they had but seldom met of late, Mr. Bragwell having moved, some years before, from Mr. Worthy's neighborhood, to a distant village, where he had bought an estate.

Mr. Bragwell was a substantial farmer and livestock owner. He had risen in the world by what worldly men call a run of good fortune. He had also been a man of great industry; that is, he had paid diligent and constant attention to his own interest. He understood business, and had a knack of turning almost everything to his own advantage. He had that sort of sense which good men call cunning, and bad men call wisdom.

He was too prudent ever to do anything so wrong that the law could take hold of him; yet he was not strict about the morality of an action, when the prospect of enriching himself by it was very great, and the chance of hurting his character was small. The corn he sent home to his customers was not always quite so good as the samples he had produced at market, and he now and then forgot to name some fault in the horses he sold at fairs. He scorned to be guilty of the petty frauds of cheating in weights and measures, for he thought that was a beggarly sin; but he valued himself on his skill in making a bargain, and fancied it showed his superior knowledge of the world to take advantage of the ignorance of a dealer.

It was his constant rule to undervalue everything he was about to buy, and to overvalue everything he was about to sell; but as he prided himself on his character, he avoided everything that was very shameful, so that he was considered merely as a hard dealer, and a keen hand at a bargain. Now and then, when he had been caught in pushing his own advantage too far, he managed to get out of the scrape by turning the whole into a jest, saying, it was a good take-in, a rare joke, and that he had only a mind to divert himself with the folly of his neighbor, who could be so easily imposed on.

Mr. Bragwell had one favorite rule, namely, that a man's success in life was a sure proof of his wisdom; and that all failure and misfortune was the consequence of a man's own foolishness. As this opinion was first taken up by him from vanity and ignorance, so it was more and more confirmed by his own prosperity. He saw that he himself had suc-ceeded greatly without either money or education to begin with, and he therefore now despised every man, however excellent his character or talents might be, who had not had the same success in life. His natural disposition was not particularly bad, but prosperity had hardened his heart. He made his own progress in life the rule by which the conduct of all other men was to be judged, without any allowance for their peculiar disadvantages, or the visitations of Providence. He thought, for his part, that every man of sense could command success on his undertakings, and control and dispose the events of his own life.

But though he considered those who had had less success than himself as no better than fools, yet he did not extend this opinion of Mr. Worthy, whom he looked upon not only as a good but wise man. They had been brought up, when children, in the same house, but with this difference, that Worthy was the nephew of the master, and Bragwell the son of the servant.

Bragwell's father had been a plowman in the family of Mr. Worthy's uncle, a sensible man, who farmed a small estate of his own, and who, having no children, brought up young Worthy as his son, instructed him in the business of farming, and at his death left him his estate.

The father of Worthy was a pious clergyman, who lived with his brother the farmer, in order to help out a narrow income. He had bestowed much pains on the instruction of his son, and frequently used to repeat to him a saying which he had picked up in a book, written by one of the greatest men in the country—that there were two things with which every man ought to be acquainted, "religion and his own business." While he therefore took care that his son should be made an excellent farmer, he filled up his leisure hours in improving his mind; so that young Worthy had read more good books, and understood them better, than most men in his station. His reading, however, had been chiefly confined to farming and divinity, the two subjects which were of the most immediate importance to him.

The reader will see, by this time, that Mr. Bragwell and Mr. Worthy were likely to be as opposite to each other as two men could well be, who were nearly of the same age and condition, and who were neither of them without credit in the world. Bragwell, indeed, made far the greater figure, for he liked to cut a dash, as he called it. And while it was the study of Worthy to conform to his position, and set a good example to those about him, it was the delight of Bragwell to contend in his way of life with men of larger fortune. He did not see how much this vanity raised the envy of his inferiors, the ill will of his equals, and the contempt of his betters.

His wife was a notable, stirring woman, but vain, violent, and ambitious, very ignorant, and very high-minded. She had married Bragwell before he was worth a shilling, and as she had brought him a good deal of money, she thought herself the grand cause of his rising in the world, and thence took occasion to govern him most completely. Whenever he ventured to oppose her, she took care to put him in mind that he owed everything to her; that had it not been for her, he might still have been stumping after a plow tail, or serving hogs in old Worthy's farmyard, but that it was she who had made a gentleman of him.

In order to set about making him a gentleman, she had begun by teasing him till he had turned away all his poor relations that worked on the farm. She next drew him off from keeping company with his old acquaintance, and at last persuaded him to leave the place where he had got his money. Poor woman! She had not sense and virtue enough to see how honorable it is for a man to raise himself in the world by fair means, and then to help forward his poor relations and friends, engaging their services by his kindness, and endeavoring to keep want out of the family.

Mrs. Bragwell was an excellent mistress according to her own notions of excellence, for no one could say that she ever lost an opportunity of scolding a servant, or was ever guilty of the weakness of overlooking a fault. Towards her two daughters her behavior was far otherwise. In them she could see nothing but perfection; but her extravagant fondness for these girls was full as much owing to pride as to affection. She was bent on making a family; and having found out that she was too ignorant, and too much trained to the habits of getting money, ever to hope to make a figure herself, she looked to her daughters as the persons who were to raise the family of the Bragwells, and in this hope she foolishly submitted to any drudgery for their sakes, and bore every kind of impertinence from them.

The first wish of her heart was to set them above their neighbors; for she used to say, what was the use of having substance, if her daughters might not carry themselves above girls who have nothing? To do her justice, she herself would be about early and late, to see that the business of the house was not neglected. She had been taught great industry, and continued to work when it was no longer necessary, both from early habit, and the desire of heaping up money for her daughters. Yet her whole notion of gentility was, that it consisted in being rich and idle; and though she was willing to be a drudge herself, she resolved to make her daughters gentlewomen on this principle. To be well dressed, and to do nothing, or nothing which is of any use, was what she fancied distinguished people in refined life.

And this is too common a notion of a fine education among some people. They do not esteem things by their use, but by their show. They estimate the value of their children's education by the money it costs, and not by the knowledge and goodness it bestows. People of this type often take pride in the expense of learning, instead of taking pleasure in the advantages of it. And the silly vanity of letting others see that they can afford anything, often sets parents on letting their daughters learn not only things of no use, but things which may be really hurtful in their situation; either by setting them above their proper duties, or by taking up their time in a way inconsistent with them.

Mrs. Bragwell sent her daughters to a boarding school, where she instructed them to hold up their heads as high as any body, to have more spirit than to be put upon by any one, never to be pitiful about money, but rather to show that they could afford to spend with the best, to keep company with the richest and most fashionable girls in the school, and to make no acquaintance with farmers' daughters.

They came home at the usual age of leaving school, with a large portion of vanity grafted on their native ignorance. The vanity was added, but the ignorance was not taken away. Of religion they could not possibly learn anything, since none was taught, for at that place it was considered as a part of education that belonged only to charity schools. Of knowledge they got just enough to laugh at their fond parents' rustic manners and vulgar language, and just enough taste to despise and ridicule every girl who was not as vainly dressed as themselves.

The mother had been comforting herself for the heavy expense of their bringing up, by looking forward to the pleasure of seeing them become fine ladies, and to the pride of marrying them above their station.

Their father hoped, also, that they would be a comfort to him both in sickness and in health. He had had no learning himself, and could write but poorly, and owed what skill he had in figures to his natural turn for business. He hoped that his daughters, after all the money he had spent on them, would now write his letters and keep his accounts. And as he was now and then laid up with a fit of the gout, he was enjoying the prospect of having two affectionate children to nurse him.

When they came home, however, he had the mortification to find that, though he had two smart showy ladies to visit him, he had neither dutiful daughters to nurse him, nor faithful stewards to keep his books, nor prudent children to manage his house. They neither soothed him by kindness when he was sick, nor helped him when he was busy. They thought the maid might take care of him in the gout, as she did before, for they fancied that nursing was a coarse and servile employment. And as to their skill in accounting, he soon found, to his cost, that though they knew how to spend pounds, shillings, and pence, yet they did not so well know how to save them.

Mrs. Bragwell one day, being very busy in preparing a great dinner for the neighbors, ventured to request her daughters to assist in making the pastry. They asked her scornfully whether she had sent them to boarding school to learn to cook, and added that they supposed she would expect them next to make puddings for the hay-makers. So saying, they coolly marched off to their music. When the mother found her girls were too polite to be of any use, she would take comfort in observing how her parlor was set out with their ornaments and flowers, their embroidery and cut paper. They spent the morning in bed, the noon in dressing, the evening at the harpsichord, and the night in reading novels.

With all these fine qualifications it is easy to suppose that, as they despised their sober duties, they no less despised their plain neighbors. When they could not get to a horse race, a petty ball, or a strolling play with some company as idle and as smart as themselves, they were driven for amusement to the library. Jack the plowboy, on whom they had now put a uniform, was employed half his time in trotting backwards and forwards, with the most wretched trash the little neighborhood bookshop could furnish. The choice was often left to Jack, who could not read, but who had general orders to bring all the new things and a great many of them.

Of the novels and plays which are so eagerly devoured by persons of this description, there is perhaps scarcely one which is not founded upon principles which would lead young women of the middle class to be discontented with their life. It is rank—it is elegance—it is beauty—it is sentimental feelings—it is sensibility—it is some needless, or some superficial, or some quality hurtful even in that fashionable person to whom the author ascribes it, which is the ruling principle. This quality, transferred into the heart and conduct of an illiterate woman in an inferior station, becomes impropriety, becomes absurdity, becomes sinfulness.

The Two Wealthy Farmers

Things were in this state, or rather growing worse, for idleness and vanity are never at a stand, when these two wealthy farmers, Bragwell and Worthy, met at Weyhill Fair, as was said before. After many hearty salutations had passed between them, it was agreed that Mr. Bragwell should spend the next day with his old friend, whose house was not many miles distant. Bragwell invited himself in the following manner: "We have not had a comfortable day's chat for years," said he, "and as I am to look at a drove of lean beasts in your neighborhood, I will take a bed at your house, and we will pass the evening in debating as we used to do. You know I always loved a bit of an argument, and am reckoned not to make the worst figure at our club; I had not, to be sure, such good learning as you had, because your father was a parson, and you got it for nothing, but I can bear my part pretty well, for all that. When any man talks to me about his learning, I ask if it has helped him to get him a good estate. If he says no, then I would not give him a rush for it; for of what use is all the learning in the world, if it does not make a man rich? But, as I was saying, I will come and see you tomorrow; but now, don't let your wife put herself into a fuss for me. Don't alter your own plain way, for I am not proud, I assure you, nor above my old friends, though, I thank God, I am pretty well in the world."

To all this flourishing speech Mr. Worthy coolly answered, "certainly worldly prosperity ought never to make any man proud, since it is God who giveth strength to get riches, and without His blessing, "'tis in vain to rise up early, and to eat the bread of carefulness.'"

About the middle of the next day, Mr. Bragwell reached Mr. Worthy's neat and pleasant dwelling. He found everything in it the reverse of his own. It had not so many ornaments, but it had more comforts. And when he saw his friend's good old-fashioned armchair, in a warm corner, he gave a sigh to think how his own had been banished to make room for his daughter's piano. Instead of made flowers in glass cases, and a tea-chest and screen too fine to be used, which he saw at home and about which he was cautioned and scolded as often as he came near them, he saw a neat shelf of good books for the service of the family, and a small medicine-chest for the benefit of the poor.

Mrs. Worthy and her daughters had prepared a plain but neat and good dinner. The tarts were so excellent that Bragwell felt a secret kind of regret that his own daughters were too refined to do anything so very useful. Indeed, he had been always unwilling to believe that anything that was very proper and every bit as necessary could be so extremely vulgar and unbecoming as his daughters were always declaring it to be. And his late experience of the little comfort he found at home inclined him now still more strongly to suspect that things were not so right there as he had been made to suppose. But it was in vain to speak, for his daughters constantly stopped his mouth by a favorite saying of theirs: "Better be out of the world, than out of the fashion."

Soon after dinner the women went out to their several employments, and Mr. Worthy being left alone with his guest, the following discourse took place:

Bragwell: "You have a couple of sober, pretty-looking girls, Worthy, but I wonder they don't quarrel a little more. Why, my girls have as much fat and flour on their heads as would half maintain my reapers in suet-pudding."

Worthy: "Mr. Bragwell, in the management of my family, I don't consider what I might afford only, though that is one great point, but I consider also what is needful and becoming in a man of my station; for there are so many useful ways of laying out money that I feel as if it were a sin to spend one unnecessary shilling. Having had the blessing of some education myself, I have been able to give the like advantage to my daughters.

"One of the best lessons I have taught them is, to know themselves; and one proof that they have learned this lesson is, that they are not above any of the duties of their station. They read and write well, and when my eyes are bad, they keep my accounts in a very pretty manner. If I had put them to learn what you call genteel things, these might either have been of no use to them, and so both time and money might have been thrown away, or they might have proved worse than nothing to them, by leading them into wrong notions and wrong company.

"Though we don't wish them to do the laborious parts of the work, yet they always assist their mother in the management of it. As to their appearance, they are every day nearly as you see them now, and on Sundays they are very neatly dressed, but it is always in a decent and modest way. There are no fringes, trimmings, and tawdry ornaments, no trains, turbans, and flounces fluttering about among my cheese and butter. And I should feel no vanity, but much mortification, if a stranger, seeing farmer Worthy's daughters at church, should ask who those fine ladies were."

Bragwell: "Now I admit I should like to have such a question asked concerning my daughters. I like to make people stare and envy. It makes one feel one's self somebody. But as to yourself, to be sure you best know what you can afford. And indeed there is some difference between your daughters and the Mrs. Bragwell."

Worthy: "For my part, before I engage in any expense, I always ask myself these two short questions: First, can I afford it? Secondly, is it proper for me?"

Bragwell: "Do you so? Now I admit I ask myself but one. For if I find I can afford it, I take care to make it proper for me. If I can pay for a thing, no one has a right to hinder me from having it."

Worthy: "Certainly; but a man's own prudence, his love of propriety, and sense of duty ought to prevent him from doing an improper thing, as

13

effectually as if there were somebody to hinder him."

Bragwell: "Now I think a man is a fool who is hindered from having anything he has a mind to— unless, he is in want of money to pay for it; I'm no friend to debt. A poor man must want on."

Worthy: "But I hope my children have learned not to want anything which is not proper for them. They are very industrious; they attend to business all day, and in the evening they sit down to their work or a good book. I think they live in the fear of God. I trust they are humble and pious, and I am sure they seem cheerful and happy. If I am sick, it is pleasant to see them dispute which shall wait on me, for they say the maid cannot do it so tenderly as themselves."

This part of the discourse staggered Bragwell. Vain as he was, he could not help feeling what a difference a religious and a worldly education made on the heart, and how much the former regulated even the natural temper. Another thing that surprised him was that these girls, living a life of domestic piety, without any public diversions, should be so very cheerful and happy, while his own daughters, who were never contradicted, and were indulged with continual amusements, were always sullen and ill tempered. That they who were more humored should be less grateful, and less happy, disturbed him much. He envied Worthy the tenderness of his children, though he would not admit it, but turned it off thus:

Bragwell: "But my girls are too smart to make mopes of, that is the truth. Though ours is such a lonely village, 'tis wonderful to see how soon they get the fashions. What with the descriptions in the magazines, they have them in a twinkling, and outdo their patterns all to nothing. I used to take the County Journal, because it was useful enough to see how oats went, the time of high water, and the price of stocks. But when my ladies came home, I was soon wheedled out of that, and forced to take a London paper that tells all about caps and feathers, and all the rubbish of the quality. When I want to know what hops are a bag, they are snatching the paper to see what violet soap is a pound. And as to the dairy, they never care how cow's milk goes, so long as they can get some stuff which they call milk of roses."

Worthy: "But do your daughters never read?"

Bragwell: "Read! I believe they do too. Why, our Jack, the plowboy, spends half his time in going to a shop in our market town, where they let out books to read with marble covers. And they sell paper with all manner of colors on the edges, and gimcracks, and powder puffs, and wash-balls, and cards without any pips, and everything in the world that's genteel and of no use. 'Twas but the other day I met Jack with a basket full of these books; so, having some time to spare, I sat down to see what they were about."

Worthy: "Well, I hope you found there what was likely to improve your daughters, and teach them the true use of time."

Bragwell: "O, as to that, you are pretty much out. I could make neither head nor tail of it. It was neither fish, flesh, nor good red herring. It was all about my lord, and Sir Harry, and the captain. But I never met with such nonsensical fellows in my life. Their talk was no more like that of my old landlord, who was a lord you know, nor the captain of our fencibles, than chalk is like cheese. I was fairly taken in at first, and began to think I had got hold of a godly book, for there was a deal about hope, and despair, and death, and heaven, and angels, and torments, and everlasting happiness. But when I got a little on, I found there was no meaning in all these words, or, if any, it was a bad meaning. Misery, it may be, only meant a disappointment about a bit of a letter; and everlasting happiness meant two people talking nonsense together for five minutes. In short, I never met with such a pack of lies.

"The people talk such gibberish as no folks in their sober senses ever did talk; and things that happen to them are not like the things that ever happen to me, or any of my acquaintance. They are at home one minute, and beyond sea the next. Beggars today, and lords tomorrow. Waiting-maids in the morning, and duchesses at night. You and I, Master Worthy, have worked hard many years, and think it very well to have scraped a trifle of money together, you a few hundreds, I suppose, and I a few thousands. But one would think every man in these books had the Bank of England in his power.

"Then there's another thing which I have never met within true life. We think it pretty well, you know, if one has got one thing, and another has got another. I'll tell you how I mean. You are reckoned sensible, our parson is learned, the squire is rich, I am rather generous, one of your daughters is pretty, and both mine are refined. But in these books—except here and there one whom they make worse than Satan himself—every man and woman's child of them are all wise, and witty, and generous, and rich, and handsome, and genteel; and all to the last degree. Nobody is middling, or good in one thing and bad in another, like my live acquaintance, but it is all up to the skies, or down to the dirt. I had rather read Tom Hickathrift, or Jack the Giant Killer, a thousand times."

Worthy: "You have found out, Mr. Bragwell, that many of these books are ridiculous. I will go farther, and say that to me they appear wicked also. And I should account the reading of them a great mischief, especially to people in middling and low life, if I only took onto the account the great loss of time such reading causes, and the aversion it leaves behind for what is more serious and solid. But this, though a bad part, is not the worst. These books give false views of human life. They teach a contempt for humble and domestic duties, for industry, frugality, and retirement. Want of youth and beauty is considered in them as ridiculous. Plain people, like you and me, are objects of contempt. Parental authority is set at naught. Nay, plots and contrivances against parents and guardians fill half the volumes.

"They consider love as the great business of human life, and even teach that it is impossible to be regulated or restrained; and to the indulgence of this passion every duty is therefore sacrificed. A country life with a kind mother or a sober aunt is described as a state of intolerable misery. And one would be apt to fancy, from their painting, that a good country-house is a prison, and a worthy father the jailer. Vice is set off with every ornament that can make it pleasing and amiable, while virtue and piety are made ridiculous by tacking to them something that is silly or absurd. Crimes that would be considered as hanging matters at the Old Bailey are here made to take the appearance of virtue, by being mixed with some wild flight of unnatural generosity. Those crying sins, adultery, gaming, duels, and self-murder, are made so familiar, and the wickedness of them is so disguised by fine words and soft descriptions, that even innocent girls get to lose their abhorrence, and to talk with complacency of things which should not be so much as named by them.

"I should not have said so much on this mischief," continued Mr. Worthy, "from which, I dare say, great folks fancy people in our station are safe enough, if I did not know and lament that this corrupt reading has now got down even among some of the lowest class. And it is an evil that is spreading every day. Poor industrious girls, who get their bread by the needle or the loom, spend half the night in listening to these books. Thus the labor of one girl is lost, and the minds of the rest are corrupted; for though their hands are employed in honest industry, which might help to preserve them from a life of sin, yet their hearts are at that very time polluted by scenes and descriptions which are too likely to plunge them into it. And I think I don't go too far when I say that the vain and showy manner in which young women who have to work for their bread, have taken to dress themselves, and the poison they draw from these books, contribute together to bring them to destruction, more than almost any other cause. Now tell me, don't you think these vile books will hurt your daughters?"

Bragwell: "Why, I do think they are grown full of schemes, and contrivances, and whispers, that's the truth on it. Everything is a secret. They always seem to be on the lookout for something; and when nothing comes on it, then they are sulky and disappointed. They will not keep company with their equals. They despise trade and farming; and, I admit, I'm for the stuff. I should not like for them to marry any but a man of substance, even if he was ever so smart. Now they will hardly sit down with a substantial country dealer. But if they hear of a recruiting party in our market town, on goes the finery; off they are. Some flimsy excuse is patched up; they want something at the bookshop, or the milliner's, because, I suppose, there is a chance that some jackanapes of an ensign may be there buying sticking plaster. In short, I do grow a little uneasy, for I should not like to see all I have saved thrown away on a knapsack."

So saying, they both rose, and walked out to view the farm. Mr. Bragwell affected greatly to admire the good order of everything he saw, but never forgot to compare it with something larger and handsomer or better of his own. It was easy to see that self was his standard of perfection in everything. All he possessed gained some increased value in his eyes, from being his; and in surveying the property of his friends, he derived food for his vanity from things which seemed least likely to raise it. Every appearance of comfort, of success, of merit, in anything that belonged to Mr. Worthy, led him to speak of some superior advantage of his own of the same kind. And it was clear that the chief part of the satisfaction he felt in walking over the farm of his friend was caused by thinking how much larger his own was.

Mr. Worthy, who felt a kindness for him that all his vanity could not cure, was on the watch how to turn their talk to some useful point; and whenever people resolve to go into company with this view, it is commonly their own fault if some opportunity of turning it to account does not offer.

He saw Bragwell was intoxicated with pride, and undone by prosperity, and that his family was in the high road to ruin. He thought that if some means could be found to open his eyes on his own character, to which he was now totally blind, it might be of the utmost service to him. The more Mr. Worthy reflected, the more he wished to undertake this kind office. He was not sure that Mr. Bragwell would bear it, but he was very sure it was his duty to attempt it. As Mr. Worthy was very humble and very candid, he had great patience and forbearance with the faults of others. He felt no pride at having escaped the same errors himself, for he knew Who it was "had made them to differ." He remembered that God had given him many advantages, a pious father, and a religious education. This made him humble under a sense of his own sins, and charitable towards the sins of others who had not had the same privileges.

Just as he was going to try to enter into a very serious conversation with his guest, he was stopped by the appearance of his daughter, who told them supper was ready.

Part 2

A CONVERSATION

Soon after supper Mrs. Worthy left the room with her daughters, at her husband's desire; for it was his intention to speak more plainly to Bragwell than was likely to be agreeable to him to hear before others.

The two farmers being seated at their little table, each in a handsome old-fashioned great chair, Bragwell began.

"It is a great comfort, neighbor Worthy, at a certain time of life, to have got above the world; my notion is, that a man should labor hard the first part of his days, and that he may then sit down and enjoy himself for the remainder. Now, though I hate boasting, yet as you are my oldest friend, I am about to open my heart to you. Let me tell you, then, I reckon I have worked as hard as any man in my time, and that I now begin to think I have a right to indulge a little. I have got my money with a good character, and I mean to spend it with credit. I pay every one his own, I set a good example, I keep to my church, I fear God, I honor the king, and I obey the laws of the land."

"This is doing a great deal, indeed," replied Mr. Worthy; "but," added he, "I doubt that more goes to the making up all these duties than men are commonly aware of. Suppose, then, that you and I talk the matter over coolly. We have the evening before us. What if we sit down together as two friends, and examine one another?"

Bragwell, who loved argument, and who was not a little vain both of his sense and his morality, accepted the challenge, and gave his word that he would take in good part anything that should be said to him.

Worthy was about to proceed, when Bragwell interrupted him for a moment, by saying, "But stop, friend. Before we begin, I wish you would remember that we have had a long walk, and I want a little refreshment. Have you no liquor that is stronger than this cider? I am afraid it will give me a fit of the gout."

Mr. Worthy immediately produced a bottle of wine, and another of liquor, saying, that though he drank neither liquor, nor even wine itself, yet his wife always kept a little of each, as a provision in case of sickness or accidents.

Farmer Bragwell preferred the brandy, and began to taste it. "Why," said he, "this is no better than English. I always use foreign myself."

"I bought this for foreign," said Mr. Worthy.

"No, no, it is English, I assure you. But I can put you into a way to get foreign nearly as cheap as English." Mr. Worthy replied that he thought that was impossible.

Bragwell: "O no, there are ways and means—a word to the wise—there is an acquaintance of mine that lives upon the south coast. You are a particular friend, and I will get you half a dozen gallons for a trifle."

Worthy: "Not if it be smuggled, Mr. Bragwell, though I should get it for sixpence a bottle."

"Ask no questions," said the other. "I never say anything to anyone, and who is the wiser?"

"And so this is your way of obeying the laws of the land," said Mr. Worthy. "Here is a fine specimen of morality."

Bragwell: "Come, come, don't make a fuss about trifles. If everyone did it, indeed, it would be another thing; but as to my getting a drop of good brandy cheap, why that can't hurt the revenue much."

Worthy: "Pray, Mr. Bragwell, what should you think of a man who would dip his hand into a bag and take out a few guineas?"

Bragwell: "Think? Why, I think that he should be hanged, to be sure."

Worthy: "But suppose that bag stood in the king's treasury."

Bragwell: "In the king's treasury! Worse and worse. What, rob the king's treasury? Well, I hope if anyone has done it, the robber will be taken up and executed, for I suppose we shall all be taxed to pay the damage."

Worthy: "Very true. If one man takes money out of the treasury, others must be obliged to pay the more into it. But what think you, if the fellow should be found to have stopped some money on its way to the treasury, instead of taking it out of the bag after it got there?"

Bragwell: "Guilty, Mr. Worthy; it is all the same, in my opinion. If I was a juryman, I should say guilty, death."

Worthy: "Hark ye, Mr. Bragwell, he that deals in smuggled brandy is the man who takes to himself the king's money on its way to the treasury, and he as much robs the government as if he dipped his hands into a bag of guineas in the treasury chamber. It comes to the same thing exactly."

Here Bragwell seemed a little offended.

"What, Mr. Worthy, do you pretend to say I am not an honest man because I like to get my brandy as cheap as I can, and because I like to save a shilling to my family? Sir, I repeat it; I do my duty to God and my neighbor. I say the Lord's prayer most days, I go to church on Sundays, I repeat my creed, and keep the Ten Commandments; and though I now and then get a little brandy cheap, yet, upon the whole, I will venture to say, I do as much as can be expected of any man."

Worthy: "Come, then, since you say you keep the commandments, you cannot be offended if I ask you whether you understand them."

Bragwell: "To be sure I do; I dare say I do. Look ye, Mr. Worthy, I don't pretend to much reading; I was not taught it, as you were. If my father had been a parson, I fancy I should have made as good a figure as some other folks; but I hope a good sense and a good heart may teach a man his duty without much scholarship."

Worthy: "To come to the point, let us now go through the commandments, and let us take along with us those explanations of them which our Saviour gave us in His Sermon on the Mount."

Bragwell: "Sermon on the Mount! Why, the Ten Commandments are in the 20th chapter of Exodus. Come, come, Mr. Worthy, I know where to find the commandments as well as you do; for it happens that I am church-warden, and I can see from the altar-piece where the Ten Commandments are without your telling me, for my pew directly faces it."

Worthy: "But I advise you to read the Sermon on the Mount, that you may see the full meaning of them."

Bragwell: "What, do you want to make me believe that there are two ways of keeping the commandments?"

Worthy: "No, but there may be two ways of understanding them."

Bragwell: "Well, I am not afraid to be put to the proof. I defy any man to say I do not keep at least all the four first that are on the left side of the altar-piece."

Worthy: "If you can prove that, I shall be more ready to believe you observe those of the other table, for he who does his duty to God will be likely to do his duty to his neighbor also."

Bragwell: "What, do you think that I serve two gods? Do you think, then, that I make graven images, and worship stocks or stones? Do you take me for an idolater?"

Worthy: "Don't triumph quite so soon, Master Bragwell. Pray, is there nothing in the world you prefer to God, and thus make an idol of? Do you not love your money, or your lands, or your crops, or your cattle, or your own will, and your own way, rather better than you love God? Do you never think of these with more pleasure than you think of Him, and follow them more eagerly than your religious duty?"

Bragwell: "O, there's nothing about that in the 20th chapter of Exodus."

Worthy: "But Jesus Christ has said, 'He that loveth father or mother more than Me is not worthy of Me.' Now it is certainly a man's duty to love his father and mother, nay, it would be wicked not to love them; and yet we must not love even these more than our Creator and our Saviour. Well, I think on this principle your heart pleads guilty to the breach of the first and second commandments. Let us proceed to the third."

Bragwell: "That is about swearing, is it not?"

Mr. Worthy, who had observed Bragwell guilty of much profaneness in using the name of his Maker—though all such offensive words have been avoided in writing this history—now told him that he had been waiting the whole day for an

28

opportunity to reprove him for his frequent breach of the third commandment.

"Good Lord, I break the third commandment!" said Bragwell. "No, indeed, hardly ever. I once used to swear a little, to be sure; but I vow I never do it now, except now and then when I happen to be angry; and in such a case, why good God, you know the sin is with those who provoke me, and not with me. Upon my soul, I don't think I have sworn an oath these three months; no, not I, faith, as I hope to be saved."

Worthy: "And yet you have broken this holy law no less than five or six times in the last speech you have made."

Bragwell: "Lord bless me! Sure you mistake. Good heavens, Mr. Worthy, I call God to witness, I have neither cursed nor sworn since I have been in the house."

Worthy: "Mr. Bragwell, this is the way in which many who call themselves very good sort of people deceive themselves. What, is it no profanation of the name of God to use it lightly, irreverently, and familiarly, as you have done? Our Saviour has not only told us not to swear by the immediate name of God, but He has said, 'Swear not at all; neither by heaven nor by the earth;' and in order to prevent our inventing any other irreligious exclamations or expressions, He has even added, 'but let your communication be yea, yea, nay, nay; for whatsoever is more than these cometh of evil.'"

Bragwell: "Well, well, I must take a little more care, I believe. I vow to heaven I did not know there had been so much harm in it, but my daughters seldom speak without using some of these words, and yet they wanted to make me believe the other day that it is monstrous vulgar to swear."

Worthy: "Women, even gentlewomen, who ought to correct this evil habit in their fathers, and husbands, and children, are too apt to encourage it by their own practice. And indeed they betray the profaneness of their own minds also by it; for none who truly venerate the holy name of God, can either profane it in this manner themselves, or hear others do so, without being exceedingly pained at it."

Bragwell: "Well, since you are so hard upon me, I believe I must even give up this point—so let us pass on to the next; and here I tread upon sure ground, for as sharp as you are upon me, you can't accuse me of being a Sabbath-breaker, since I go to church every Sunday of my life, unless on some very extraordinary occasion."

Worthy: "For those occasions the gospel allows, by saying, 'The Sabbath was made for man, and not man for the Sabbath.' Our own sickness, or attending on the sickness of others are lawful impediments."

Bragwell: "Yes, and I am now and then obliged to look at a drove of beasts, or to go a journey; or to take some medicine, or perhaps some friend may call upon me, or it may be very cold, or very hot, or very rainy."

Worthy: "Poor excuses, Mr. Bragwell; I am afraid these will not pass on the day of judgment. But how is the rest of your Sunday spent?"

Bragwell: "O, why, I assure you I often go to church in the afternoon also, and even if I am ever so sleepy."

Worthy: "And so you finish your nap at church, I suppose."

Bragwell: "Why, as to that, to be sure we do contrive to have something a little nicer than common for dinner on a Sunday, in consequence of which one eats, you know, a little more than ordinary; and having nothing to do on that day, one has more leisure to take a cheerful glass; and all these things will make one a little heavy, you know."

Worthy: "And don't you take a little ride in the morning and look at your sheep, when the weather is good, and so fill your mind just before you go to church with thoughts of them; and when you come away again, don't you settle an account or write a few letters of business?"

Bragwell: "I can't say but I do; but that is nothing to any body, as long as I set a good example by keeping to my church."

Worthy: "And how do you pass your Sunday evenings?"

Bragwell: "My wife and daughters go a visiting of a Sunday afternoon. My daughters are glad to get out at any rate, and as to my wife, she says that being ready dressed it is a pity to lose the opportunity; besides, it saves her time on a weekday;

so then you see I have it all my own way, and when I have got rid of the ladies, who are ready to faint at the smell of tobacco, I can venture to smoke a pipe, and drink a sober glass of punch with half a dozen friends."

Worthy: "Which punch being made of smuggled brandy, and drank on the Lord's day in very vain as well as profane and worldly company, you are enabled to break both the law of God and that of your country at a stroke. And I suppose that when you are together, you speak of your cattle, or of your crops, after which, perhaps you talk over a few of your neighbors' faults, and then you brag a little of your own wealth, or your own achievements."

Bragwell: "Why, you seem to know us so well, that any one would think you had been sitting behind the curtain; and yet you are a little mistaken too, for I think we have hardly said a word for several of our last Sundays on anything but politics."

Worthy: "And do you find that you much improve your Christian charity by that subject?"

Bragwell: "Why, to be sure, we do quarrel till we are very near fighting, that is the worst of it."

Worthy: "And then you call names, and swear a little, I suppose."

Bragwell: "Why, when one is contradicted and put in a passion, you know, flesh and blood can't bear it."

Worthy: "And when all your friends have gone home, what becomes of the rest of the evening?"

Bragwell: "That is just as it happens; sometimes I read the newspaper; and as one is generally most tired on the days one does nothing, I go to bed earlier than on other days, that I may be more fit to get up to my business the next morning."

Worthy: "So you shorten Sunday as much as you can, by cutting off a bit at both ends, I suppose; for I take it for granted, you lie a little later in the morning."

Bragwell: "Come, come, we sha'n't get through the whole ten tonight, if you stand quibbling at this rate. You may pass over the fifth, for my father and mother have been dead since I was a boy, so I am clear of that scrape."

Worthy: "There are, however, many relative duties in that commandment; unkindness to all kindred is forbidden."

Bragwell: "O, if you mean my turning off my nephew Tom, the plowboy, you must not blame me for that; it was all my wife's fault. He was as good a lad as ever lived, to be sure, and my own brother's boy; but my wife could not bear that a boy in a servant's coat should be about the house calling her aunt. We quarreled like dog and cat about it; and when he was turned away, she and I did not speak for a week."

Worthy: "Which was a fresh breach of the commandment; a worthy nephew turned out of doors, and a wife not spoken to for a week, are not very convincing proofs of your observance of the fifth commandment."

Bragwell: "Well, I long to come to the sixth, for you don't think I commit murder, I hope."

Worthy: "I am not sure of that."

Bragwell: "What, I kill any body?"

Worthy: "Why, the laws of the land, indeed, and the disgrace attending it, are almost enough to keep any man from actual murder; let me ask, however, do you never give way to unjust anger, and passion, and revenge? As, for instance, do you never feel your resentment kindle against some of the politicians who contradict you on a Sunday night; and do you never push your animosity against somebody that has affronted you, further than the occasion will justify?"

Bragwell: "Hark ye, Mr. Worthy, I am a man of substance, and nobody shall offend me without my being even with him. So as to injuring a man, if he affronts me first, there's nothing but good reason in that."

Worthy: "Very well; only bear in mind that you willfully break this commandment, whether you abuse your servant, are angry at your wife, watch for a moment to revenge an injury on your neighbor, or even wreak your passion on a harmless beast, for you have then the seeds of murder working in your breast. And if there were no law, no death penalty to check you, and no fear of disgrace neither, I am not sure where you would stop."

Bragwell: "Why, Mr. Worthy, you have a strange way of explaining the commandments! So you set me down for a murderer, merely because I bear hatred to a man who has done me a hurt, and am glad to do him a like injury in my turn—I am sure I should lack spirit if I did not."

Worthy: "I go by the Scripture rule, which says, 'He that hateth his brother is a murderer;' and again, 'Love your enemies; bless them that curse you, and pray for them that despitefully use you, and persecute you.' Besides, Mr. Bragwell, you made it a part of your boast that you said the Lord's prayer every day, wherein you pray to God to forgive you your trespasses as you forgive them that trespass against you. If, therefore, you do not forgive them that trespass against you, in that case you pray daily that your own trespasses may never be forgiven."

Bragwell: "Well, come, let us make haste and get through these commandments. The next is, 'Thou shalt not commit adultery.' Thank God, neither I nor my family can be said to break the seventh commandment."

Worthy: "Here again, remember how Christ Himself hath said, 'Whosoever looketh on a woman to lust after her, hath committed adultery with her already in his heart.' These are no farfetched expressions of mine, Mr. Bragwell; they are the words of Jesus Christ. I hope you will not charge Him with having carried things too far; for, if you do, you charge Him with being mistaken in the religion He taught, and this can only be accounted for by supposing Him an imposter."

Bragwell: "Why, upon my word, Mr. Worthy, I don't like these sayings of His, which you quote upon me so often, and that is the truth of it; and I can't say I feel much disposed to believe them."

Worthy: "I hope you believe in Jesus Christ. I hope you believe that creed of yours, which you also boasted of repeating so regularly."

Bragwell: "Well, well, I'll believe anything you say, rather than stand quarrelling with you."

Worthy: "I hope, then, you will allow, that since it is committing adultery to look at a woman with even an irregular thought, it follows from the same rule, that all immodest dress in your daughters, or indecent jests and double meaning in yourself—all loose songs or novels, and all diversions also which have a like dangerous tendency, are forbidden by the seventh commandment; for it is most plain, from what Christ has said, that it takes in not only the act but the inclination, the desire, the indulged imagination. The act is only the last and highest degree of any sin, the topmost round, as it were, of a ladder, to which all the lower rounds are only as so many steps and stages."

Bragwell: "Strict indeed, Mr. Worthy, but let us go on to the next. You won't pretend to say I steal. Mr. Bragwell, I trust, was never known to rob on the highway, to break open his neighbor's house, or to use false weights or measures."

Worthy: "No, nor have you ever been under any temptation to do it, and yet there are a thousand ways of breaking the eighth commandment besides actual stealing. For instance, do you never hide the faults of the goods you sell, and heighten the faults of those you buy? Do you never take advantage of an ignorant dealer, and ask more for a thing than it is worth? Do you never turn the distressed circumstances of a man who has something to sell, to your own unfair benefit, and thus act as unjustly by him as if you had stolen? Do you never cut off a shilling from a workman's wages, under a pretense that your conscience can't justify? Do you never pass off an unsound horse for a sound one? Do you never conceal the real rent of your estate from the overseers, and thereby rob the poor-rates of their legal due?"

Bragwell: "Pooh! These things are done every day. I sha'n't go to set up for being better than my neighbors in this sort of thing; these little matters will pass muster—I don't set up for a reformer. If I am as good as the rest of my neighbors, no man can call me to account. I am not worse, I trust, and I don't pretend to be better."

Worthy: "You must be tried hereafter at the bar of God, and not by a jury of your fellow creatures; and the Scriptures are given us, in order to show by what rule we shall be judged. How many or how few do as you do, is quite aside from the question. Jesus Christ has even told us to strive to enter in at the strait gate, so that we ought rather to take fright from our being like the common run of people, than to take comfort from our being so."

Bragwell: "Come, I don't like all this close work. It makes a man feel, I don't know how; I don't find myself as happy as I did—I don't like this fishing in troubled waters—I'm as merry as the day is long when I let these things alone. I'm glad we have got to the ninth. But I suppose I shall be lugged in there too, head and shoulders. Anyone who did not know me would really think I was a great sinner, by your way of putting things. I don't bear false witness, however."

Worthy: "You mean, I suppose, you would not swear a man's life away falsely before a magistrate; but do you take equal care not to slander or backbite him? Do you never represent a good action of a man you have quarreled with as if it were a bad one; or do you never make a bad one worse than it is by your manner of telling it? Even when you invent no false circumstances, do you never give such a color to those you relate, as to leave a false impression on the mind of the hearers? Do you never twist a story so as to make it tell a little better for yourself, and a little worse for your neighbor, than truth and justice warrant?"

Bragwell: "Why, as to that matter, all this is only natural."

Worthy: "Aye, much too natural to be right, I doubt. Well, now we have got to the last of the commandments."

Bragwell: "Yes, I have run the gauntlet through them all You will bring me in guilty here, I suppose, for the pleasure of going through with it; for you condemn without judge or jury, Master Worthy."

Worthy: "The culprit, I think, has hitherto pleaded guilty to the evidence brought against him. The tenth commandment, however, goes to the root and principle of evil; it dives to the bottom of things. This command checks the first rising of sin in the heart, teaches us to strangle it in the birth, as it were, before it breaks out in those acts which are forbidden; as for instance, every man covets before he proceeds to steal. Nay, many covet, who dare not steal lest they should suffer for it."

Bragwell: "Why, look ye, Mr. Worthy, I don't understand these new-fashioned explanations. One would not have a grain of sheer goodness left if everything one does is to be frittered away at this rate. I am not, I admit, quite so good as I thought; but if what you say were true, I should be so miserable I should not know what to do with myself. Why, I tell you, all the world may be said to break the commandments, at this rate."

Worthy: "Very true. The entire world, and I myself also, are but too apt to break them, if not in the letter, at least in the spirit of them. So, then, all the world is, as the Scripture expresses it, 'guilty before God;' and if guilty, they should own they are guilty, and not stand up and justify themselves as you do, Mr. Bragwell."

Bragwell: "Well, according to my notion, I am a very honest man, and honesty is the sum and substance of all religion, say I."

Worthy: "All truth, honesty, justice, order, and obedience, grow out of the Christian religion. The true Christian acts, at all times and on all occasions, from the pure and spiritual principle of love to God. On this principle, he is upright in his dealings, true to his word, kind to the poor, helpful to the oppressed. In short, if he truly loves God, he must do justice, and can't help loving mercy. Christianity is a uniform, consistent thing. It does not allow us to make up for the breach of one part of God's law by our strictness in observing another. There is no sponge in one duty that can wipe out the spot of another sin."

Bragwell: "Well, but at this rate I should be always puzzling and blundering, and should never know for certain whether I was right or not; whereas I am now quite satisfied with myself, and have no doubts to torment me."

Worthy: "One way of knowing whether we really desire to obey the whole law of God, is this: when we find we have as great a regard to that part of it, the breach of which does not touch our own interest, as to that part which does. For instance, a man robs me; I am in a violent anger with him, and when it is said to me, 'Doest thou well to be angry?' I answer, 'I do well. "Thou shalt not steal" is a law of God, and this fellow has broken that law.' Aye, but says conscience, "Tis thy own property which is in question. He has broken thy hedge—he has stolen thy sheep—he has taken thy purse. Art thou, therefore, sure whether it is his violation of thy property, or of God's law, which provokes thee?'

"I will put a second case. I hear another swear most grievously; or I meet him coming drunk out of an alehouse; or I find him singing a loose, profane song. If I am not as much grieved for this blasphemer, or this drunkard, as I was for the robber—if I do not take the same pains to bring him to a sense of his sin, which I did to bring the robber to justice, 'how dwelleth the love of God in me?' Is it not clear that I value my own sheep more than God's commandments—that I prize my purse more than I love my Maker? In short, whenever I find out that I am more jealous for my own property than for God's law—more careful about my own reputation than His honor, I always suspect I am upon wrong ground, and that even my right actions are not proceeding from a right principle."

Bragwell: "Why, what in the world would you have me do?"

"Worthy: "You must confess that your sins are sins. You must not merely call them sins, while you see no guilt in them, but you must confess them so as to hate and detest them—so as to be habitually humbled under the sense of them—so as to trust for salvation, not in your freedom from them, but in the mercy of a Saviour—and so as to make it the chief business of your life to contend against them, and in the main to forsake them. And remember that if you seek for a deceitful gaiety, rather than a well-grounded cheerfulness—if you prefer a false security to final safety, and now go away to your cattle and your farm, and dismiss the subject from your thoughts lest it should make you uneasy, I am not sure that this simple discourse may not appear against you at the day of account as a fresh proof that you 'loved darkness rather than light,' and so increase your condemnation."

Mr. Bragwell was more affected than he cared to admit. He went to bed with less spirit and more humility than usual. He did not, however, care to let Mr. Worthy see the impression which had been made upon him. At parting next morning, he shook him by the hand more cordially than usual, and made him promise to return his visit in a short time.

Part 3

THE VISIT RETURNED

Mr. Bragwell, when he returned home from his visit to Mr. Worthy, as recorded in the second part of this history, found that he was not quite so happy as he had formerly been. The discourses of Mr. Worthy had broken in not a little on his comfort. And he began to suspect that he was not so completely in the right as his vanity had led him to believe. He seemed also to feel less satisfaction in the idle gentility of his own daughters, since he had been witness to the simplicity, modesty, and usefulness of those of Mr. Worthy. And he could not help seeing that the vulgar violence of his wife did not produce so much family happiness at home as the humble piety and quiet diligence of Mrs. Worthy produced in the house of his friend.

Happy would it have been for Mr. Bragwell if he had followed up these new convictions of his own mind, which would have led him to struggle against the power of evil principles in himself, and to control the force of evil habits in his family. But his convictions were just strong enough to make him uneasy under his errors, without driving him to reform them. The slight impressions soon wore off, and he fell back into his old practices.

Still, his esteem for Mr. Worthy was not at all abated by the plain dealing of that honest friend. It is true he dreaded his piercing eye. He felt that his example held out a constant reproof to himself. Yet such is the force of early affection and rooted reverence that he longed to see him at his house. This desire, indeed, as is commonly the case, was made up of mixed motives. He wished for the pleasure of his friend's company; he longed for that favorite triumph of a vulgar mind, an opportunity of showing him his riches; and he thought it would raise his credit in the world to have a man of Mr. Worthy's character at his house.

Mr. Bragwell, it is true, still went on with the same eagerness in gaining money, and the same display in spending it. But though he was as covetous as ever, he was not quite so sure that it was right to be so. While he was actually engaged abroad, indeed, in transactions with his dealers, he was not very scrupulous about the means by which he got his money; and while he was indulging in festivity with his friends at home, he was easy enough as to the manner in which he spent it.

But a man can neither be making bargains, nor making feasts, always; there must be some intervals between these two great objects for which worldly men may be said to live; and in some of these intervals, the most worldly form perhaps some random plans of amendment. And though many a one may say, in the fullness of enjoyment, "Soul, take thine ease; eat, drink, and be merry;" yet hardly any man, perhaps, allows himself to say, even in the most secret moments, I will never retire from business—I will never repent—I will never think of death—eternity shall never come into my thoughts. The most that such a one probably ventures to say is, I need not repent yet; I will continue such a sin a little longer; it will be time enough to think on the next world when I am no longer fit for the business or the pleasures of this.

Such was the case with Bragwell. He set up, in his own mind, a general distant sort of resolution that some years hence, when he should be a few years older, and a few thousands richer—when a few more of his present schemes were completed, he would then think of altering his course of life. He would then certainly set about spending a religious old age; he would reform some practices in his dealings, or perhaps quit business entirely; he would think about reading good books, and when he had completed such and such a purchase, he would even begin to give something to the poor, but at present he really had little to spare for charity. The very reason why he should have given more was just the cause he assigned for not giving at all, namely, the hardness of the times. The true, grand source of charity, self-denial, never came into his head. Spend less, that you may save more, he would have thought a shrewd idea enough; but spend less, that you may spare more, never entered into his book of proverbs.

At length the time came when Mr. Worthy had promised to return his visit. It was indeed a little hastened by the notice that Mr. Bragwell would have, in the course of the week, a piece of land to sell by auction; and though Mr. Worthy believed the price was likely to be above his pocket, yet he knew it was an occasion which would be likely to bring the principal farmers of that neighborhood together, some of whom he wanted to meet. And it was on this occasion that Mr. Bragwell prided himself that he should show his neighbors so sensible a man as his dear friend Mr. Worthy.

Worthy arrived at his friend's house on Saturday, time enough to see the house, and garden, and grounds of Mr. Bragwell by daylight. He saw with pleasure those evident signs of his friend's prosperity, for he had a warm and generous heart; but as he was a man of a sober mind, and was a most exact dealer in truth, he never allowed his tongue the license of immodest commendation, which he used to say either savored of flattery or envy. Indeed, he never rated mere worldly things so high as to bestow upon them undue praise.

His calm approval somewhat disappointed the vanity of Mr. Bragwell, who could not help secretly suspecting that his friend, as good a man as he was, not quite free from envy. He felt, however, very much inclined to forgive this jealousy, which he feared the sight of his ample property and handsome habitation must naturally awaken in the mind of a man whose own possessions were so inferior. He practiced the usual trick of ordinary and vulgar minds, that of pretending to find some fault with those things that particularly deserved praise, when he found Mr. Worthy disposed to pass them over in silence.

When they came in to supper, he affected to talk of the comforts of Mr. Worthy's little parlor, by way of calling his attention to his own large one. He repeated the word snug, as applied to everything at Mr. Worthy's, with the plain design to make comparisons favorable to his own more ample domains. He contrived, as he passed to his chair, by a seeming accident, to push open the door of a large buffet in the parlor, in which all the finery was most ostentatiously set out to view. He protested with a look of satisfaction which belied his words, that for his part he did not care a bit for all this display, and then smiling and rubbing his hands, added with an air of no small importance, "What a good thing it is, though, for people of substance, that the tax on plate is taken off. You are a happy man, Mr. Worthy, you do not feel these things; tax or no tax is all the same to you." He took care during this speech, by a cast of his eye, to direct Mr. Worthy's attention to a great profusion of the brightest cups, salvers, and tankards, and other shining ornaments that crowded the buffet.

Mr. Worthy gravely answered, "Mr. Bragwell, it was indeed a tax which could not affect so plain a man as myself, but as it fell on a mere luxury, and therefore could not hurt the poor, I was always sorry that it could not be made productive enough to be continued. A man in my middling situation, who is contented with a good glass of beer, poured from a handsome earthen mug, the glass, the mug, and the beer, all of English manufacture, will be but little disturbed at taxes on plate or on wine; but he will regret, as I do, that many of these taxes are so much evaded that new taxes are continually brought on to make up the deficiencies of the old."

During supper the young ladies sat in disdainful silence, not thinking it fit to bestow the smallest civility on so plain a man as Mr. Worthy. They left the room with their mamma as soon as possible, being impatient to get away to ridicule their father's old-fashioned friend at full liberty.

THE DANCE, OR THE CHRISTMAS MERRY-MAKING

As soon as they were gone, Mr. Worthy asked Bragwell how his family comforts stood, and how his daughters, who he said were really fine young women, went on.

"O, as to that," replied Bragwell, "pretty much like other men's handsome daughters, I suppose, that is, worse and worse. I really begin to apprehend that their fantastical notions have gained such a head, that after all the money I have scraped together, I shall never get them well married. Betsy has just lost as good an offer as any girl could desire, young Wilson, as honest and substantial a grazier as any in the country. He not only knows everything proper for his station, but also is pleasing in his behavior, and a pretty scholar into the bargain; he reads history books and voyages of a winter's evening to his infirm father, instead of going to the card-assembly in our town. He neither likes drinking nor sporting, and is a sort of favorite with our parson, because he takes in the weekly numbers of a fine Bible with cuts, and subscribes to the Sunday-school, and makes a fuss about helping the poor, these dear times as they call them, but I think they are good times for us, Mr. Worthy.

"Well, for all this, Betsy only despised him, and laughed at him; but as he is both handsome and rich, I thought she might come round at last, and so I invited him to come and stay a day or two at Christmas, when we have always a little sort of merry-making here. But it would not do. He refused to talk in the vain manner that she has been used to in the marble-covered books I told you of. He told her, indeed, that it would be the happiness of his heart to live with her, which I admit I thought was as much as could be expected of any man; but she had no notion of marrying one who was only desirous of living with her. No, no, her lover must declare himself ready to die for her, which honest Wilson was not such a fool as to offer to do. In the afternoon, however, he got a little into her favor by making out a riddle or two in the Lady's Diary, and she condescended to say she did not think Mr.

Wilson had been so good a scholar; but he soon spoiled all again.

"We had a little dance in the evening. The young man, though he had not much taste for that sort of thing, yet thought he could foot it a little in the old-fashioned way, so he asked Betsy to be his partner. But when he asked what dance they should call, she drew up her head, and in a strange gibberish, said she should dance nothing but a *Minuet de la Cour,* and ordered him to call it. Wilson stared, and honestly told her she must call it herself, for he could neither spell nor pronounce such outlandish words. I burst out laughing, and told him I supposed it was something like questions and command, and if so, that was much merrier than dancing. Seeing her partner standing stock still, and not knowing how to get out of the scrape, the girl began by herself, and fell to swimming, and sinking, and capering, and flourishing, and posturing, for all the world just like the man on the slack rope at our fair. But seeing Wilson staring like a stuck pig, and we all laughing at her, she resolved to inflict her malice upon him; so, with a look of rage and disdain, she advised him to go down country bumpkin with the dairy-maid, who would make a much fitter partner, as well as wife for him, than she could do.

"'I am quite of your mind, Miss,' said he, with more spirit than I thought was in him; 'you may make a good partner for a dance, but you would make a sad one to go through life with. I will take my leave of you, Miss, with this short story. I had lately a pretty large concern in hay jobbing, which took me to London. I waited a good while in the hay-market for my dealer, and to pass away the time, I stepped into a sort of singing play-house there, where I was grieved to the heart to see young women painted and decked out, and capering away just as you have been doing. I thought it bad enough in them, and wondered the quality could be entertained with such indecent mummery; but little did I think to meet with the same paint, finery, and tricks in a farmhouse. I will never marry a woman who despises me or the station in which I should place her, and so I take my leave.' Poor girl, how she was provoked! To be publicly refused, and turned off as it were, by a grazier! But it was of use to some of the other girls, who have not held up their heads quite so high since, nor painted quite so red, but have condescended to speak to their equals.

"But how I run on. I forget it is Saturday night, and that I ought to be paying my workmen, who are all waiting for me outside."

SATURDAY NIGHT,
OR THE WORKMEN'S WAGES

As soon as Mr. Bragwell had done paying his men, Mr. Worthy said to him, "I have made it a habit, and I hope not an unprofitable one, of trying to turn to some moral use, not only all the events of daily life, but all the employments of it too. And though it occurs so often, I hardly know one that sets me to thinking more seriously than the ordinary business you have just been discharging."

"Aye," said Bragwell, "it sets me thinking too, and seriously, as you say, when I observe how much the price of wages is increased."

"Yes, yes, you are ready enough to think of that," said Worthy, "but you say not a word of how much the value of your land is increased, and that the more you pay the more you can afford to pay. But the thoughts I spoke of are quite of another kind. When I call in my laborers on a Saturday night to pay them, it often brings to my mind the great and general day of account, when I, and you, and all of us shall be called to our grand and awful reckoning, when we shall go to receive our wages, master and servant, farmer and laborer.

"When I see that one of my men has failed of the wages he should have received, because he has been idling at a fair; another has lost a day by a drinking-bout; a third confesses that though he had task-work and might have earned still more, yet he has been careless and has not his full pay to receive; this, I say, sometimes sets me to thinking whether I also have made the most of my time. And when I come to pay even the more diligent who have worked all the week, when I reflect that even these have done no more than it was their duty to do, I cannot help saying to myself, night is come— Saturday night is come. No repentance, or diligence on the part of these poor men can now make a bad week's work good. This week is gone into eternity. Tomorrow is the season of rest; working time is over. My life also will soon be swallowed up in eternity; soon the space allotted me for diligence, for labor, will be over. Soon will the grand question be asked, 'What hast thou done? Didst thou use thy working-days to the end for which they were given?' With some such thoughts I commonly go to bed, and they help to quicken me to a keener diligence for the next week."

SOME ACCOUNT
OF A SUNDAY IN
MR. BRAGWELL'S FAMILY

Mr. Worthy had been for so many years used to the sober ways of his own well-ordered family that he greatly disliked passing a Sunday in any house of which religion was not the governing principle. Indeed, he commonly ordered his affairs and regulated his journeys with an eye to this object. "To pass a Sunday in an irreligious family," said he, "is always unpleasant, often unsafe. I seldom find I can do them any good, and they may perhaps do me some harm. At least, I am giving a sanction to their manner of passing, if I pass it in the same manner. If I reprove them, I subject myself to the charge of singularity, and of being 'righteous overmuch.' If I do not reprove them, I confirm and strengthen them in evil. And whether I reprove them or not, I certainly partake of their guilt if I spend it as they do."

He had, however, so strong a desire to be useful to Mr. Bragwell that he at length determined to break through his common practice, and pass the Sunday at his house. Mr. Worthy was surprised to find that, though the church-bell was going, the breakfast was not ready, and expressed his wonder how this should be the case in so industrious a family. Bragwell made some awkward excuses. He said his wife worked her servants so hard all the week that even she, as notable as she was, a little relaxed from the strictness of her demands on Sunday mornings; and he admitted that, in a general way, no one was up early enough for church. He confessed that his wife commonly spent the morning in making puddings, pies, and cakes, to last through the week, as Sunday was the only leisure time she and her maids had. Mr. Worthy soon saw an uncommon bustle in the house. All hands were busy. It was nothing but baking and boiling, and frying and roasting, and running, and scolding, and eating. The boy was kept from church to clean the plate, the man to gather the fruit, the mistress to make the cheese cakes, the maids to dress the dinner, and the young ladies to dress themselves.

The truth was, Mrs. Bragwell, who had heard much of the order and good management of Mr. Worthy's family, but who looked down with disdain upon them as far less rich than herself, was resolved to indulge her vanity on the present occasion. She was determined to be even with Mrs. Worthy, in whose praises Bragwell had been so loud, and felt no small pleasure in the hope of making her guest uneasy in comparing her with his own wife, when he should be struck dumb with the display both of her skill and her wealth.

Mr. Worthy was indeed struck to behold as large a dinner as he had been used to see at a justices' meeting. He, whose frugal and pious wife had accustomed him only to such a plain Sunday's dinner as could be prepared without keeping any one from church, when he surveyed the loaded table of his friend, instead of feeling that envy which these grand preparations were meant to raise, felt nothing but disgust at the vanity of his friend's wife, mixed with much thankfulness for the piety and simplicity of his own.

After having made the dinner wait a long time, the Misses Bragwell marched in, dressed as if they were going to a party; they looked very scornfully at having been so hurried, though they had been dressing ever since they got up; and their fond father, when he saw them so fine, forgave all their impertinence, and cast an eye of triumph on Mr. Worthy, who felt he had never loved his own humble daughters so well as at that moment.

In the afternoon the whole party went to church. To do them justice, it was indeed their common practice once a day, when the weather was good, and the road was neither dusty nor dirty, when the minister did not begin too early, when the young ladies had not been disappointed of their new bonnets on the Saturday night, and when they had no smart company in the house who rather wished to stay at home. When this last was the case, which, to say the truth, happened pretty often, it was thought a piece of good manners to conform to the humor of the guests. Mr. Bragwell had this day not had any of his usual company, well knowing that their vain and worldly conversation would only serve to draw on him some new reprimand from his friend.

Mrs. Bragwell and her daughters picked up, as usual, a good deal of acquaintance at church. Many compliments passed, and much of the news of the week was related before the service began. They waited with impatience for the reading the lessons as a license for whispering; and the subject begun during the lessons was finished while they were singing. The young ladies made an appointment for the afternoon with a friend in the next pew, while their mamma took the opportunity of inquiring the character of a dairy-maid, which, she observed with a compliment to her own good management, would save time on a week-day.

Mr. Worthy, who found himself quite in a new world, returned home with his friend alone. In the evening he ventured to ask Bragwell if he did not, on a Sunday night at least, make it a custom to read and pray with his family. Bragwell told him he was sorry to say he had no family at home, else he should like

56

to do it for the sake of example. But as his servants worked hard all the week, his wife was of the opinion that they should have a little holiday.

Mr. Worthy pressed it home upon him whether the utter neglect of his servants' principles was not likely to make a heavy article in his final account, and asked him if he did not believe that the too general liberty of meeting together, jaunting, and diverting themselves on Sunday evenings, was not often found to produce the worst effects on the morals of servants, and the good order of families.

"I put it to your conscience," said he, "Mr. Bragwell, whether Sunday, which was meant as a blessing and a benefit, is not, as it is commonly kept, turned into the most mischievous part of the week, by the selfish kindness of masters, who not daring to set their servants about any public work, allot them that day to follow their own devices, that they themselves may, with more rigor, refuse them a little indulgence and a reasonable holiday in the working part of the week, which a good servant has now and then a fair right to expect. Those masters who will give them half or all the Lord's day, will not spare them a single hour of a working-day. Their work must be done; God's work may be let alone."

Mr. Bragwell agreed that Sunday had produced many mischiefs in his own family, that the young men and maids, having no eye upon them, frequently went to improper places with other servants turned adrift like them, that in these parties the poor girls were too frequently led astray, and the men got to public houses, and fives-playing. But it was none of his business to watch them. His family only did as others do; indeed, it was his wife's concern, and as she was so good a manager on other days that she would not spare them an hour to visit a sick father or mother, it would be hard, she said, if they might not have Sunday afternoon to themselves, and she could not blame them for making the most of it.

Indeed, she was so indulgent in this particular that she often excused the men from going to church, that they might serve the beasts, and the maids that they might get the milking done before the holiday part of the evening came on. She would not indeed hear of any competition between doing her work and taking their pleasure; but when the difference lay between their going to church and taking their pleasure, he must say that for his wife, she always inclined to the good-natured side of the question. She is strict enough in keeping them sober, because drunkenness is a costly sin; and, to do her justice, she does not care how little they sin at her expense.

"Well," said Mr. Worthy, "I always like to examine both sides fairly, and to see the different effects of opposite practices. Now, which plan produces the greatest share of comfort to the master, and of profit to the servants, in the long run? Your servants, it's likely, are very much attached to you, and very fond of living where they get their own way in so great a point."

"O, as to that," replied Bragwell, "you are quite wrong. My house is a scene of discord, mutiny, and discontent. And though there is not a better manager in England than my wife, yet she is always changing her servants, so that every quarter-day is a sort of jail-delivery at my house; and when they go off, as they often do, at a moment's warning, to tell the truth, I often give them money privately, that they may not carry my wife before the justice to get their wages."

"I see," said Mr. Worthy, "that all your worldly compliances do not procure you even worldly happiness. As to my own family, I take care to let them see that their pleasure is bound up with their duty, and that what they may call my strictness has nothing in view but their safety and happiness. By this means, I commonly gain their love, as well as secure their obedience. I know that with all my care I am liable to be disappointed, 'from the corruption that is in the world through sin.' But whenever this happens, so far from encouraging me in carelessness, it only serves to quicken my zeal. If, by God's blessing, my servant turns out a good Christian, I have been an humble instrument in His hand of saving a soul committed to my charge."

Mrs. Bragwell came home, but brought only one of her daughters with her; the other, she said, had given them the slip, and gone with a young friend, and would not return for a day or two. Mr. Bragwell was greatly displeased, as he knew that young friend had but a slight character, and kept bad acquaintances. Mrs. Bragwell came in, all hurry and bustle, saying, if her family did not go to bed with the lamb on Sundays, when they had nothing to do, how could they rise with the lark on Mondays, when so much was to be done?

Mr. Worthy had this night much matter for reflection. "We need not," said he, "go into the great world to look for dissipation and vanity; we can find both in a farm-house. 'As for me, and my house,'" continued he, "'we will serve the Lord' every day, but especially on the Sabbath. It 'is the day which the Lord hath made'—hath made for Himself; 'we will rejoice in it,' and consider the religious use of it not only as a duty but as a privilege."

The next morning Mr. Bragwell and his friend set out early for the Golden Lion. What passed on this little journey, my readers shall hear soon.

Part 4

THE SUBJECT OF PRAYER DISCUSSED IN A MORNING'S RIDE

It was mentioned in the last part of this history that the chief reason which had drawn Mr. Worthy to visit his friend just at the present time was that Mr. Bragwell had a small estate to sell by auction. Mr. Worthy, though he did not think he should be a bidder, wished to be present, as he had business to settle with one or two persons who were expected at the Golden Lion on that day, and he had put off his visit till he had seen the sale advertised in the county paper.

Mr. Bragwell and Mr. Worthy set out early on Monday morning, on their way to the Golden Lion, a small inn in a neighboring market town. As they had time before them, they had agreed to ride slowly, that they might converse on some useful subject; but here, as usual, they had two opinions about the same thing. Mr. Bragwell's notion of a useful subject was something by which money was to be got, and a good bargain struck.

Mr. Worthy was not less a man of business than his friend. His schemes were wise, and his calculations just; his reputation for integrity and good sense made him the common judge and umpire in his neighbors' affairs, while no one paid a more exact attention to every transaction of his own. But the business of getting money was not with him the first, much less was it the whole concern of the day. Every morning when he rose, he remembered that he had a Maker to worship as well as a family to maintain.

Religion, however, never made him neglect business, though it sometimes led him to postpone it. He used to say, no man had any reason to expect God's blessing through the day, who did not ask it in the morning; nor was he likely to spend the day in the fear of God, who did not begin it with His worship. But he had not the less sense, spirit, and activity, when he was among men abroad, because he had first served God at home.

As these two farmers rode along, Mr. Worthy took occasion, from the fineness of the day and the beauty of the country through which they passed, to turn the discourse to the goodness of God, and our infinite obligations to Him. He knew that the transition from thanksgiving to prayer would be natural and easy, and he therefore, sliding by degrees into that important subject, observed that secret prayer was a duty of universal obligation which every man had it in his power to fulfill, and which he seriously believed was the groundwork of all religious practice, and of all devout affections.

Mr. Bragwell felt conscious that he was very negligent and irregular in the performance of this duty; indeed, he considered it as a mere ceremony, or at least as a duty which might give way to the slightest temptation of drowsiness at night, or of business in the morning. As he knew he did not live in the conscientious performance of this practice, he tried to ward off the subject, knowing what an honest way his friend had of putting things. After some evasion, he at last said he certainly thought private prayer a good custom, especially for people who have time, and that those who were sick, or old, or out of business, could not do better, but that, for his part, he believed much of this sort of thing was not expected from men in active life.

Worthy: "I should think, Mr. Bragwell, that those who are most exposed to temptation stand most in need of prayer. Now there are few, I think, who are more exposed to temptation than men in business, for those must be in most danger, at least from the world, who have most to do with it. And if this be true, ought we not to prepare ourselves in prayer for the trials of the market, the field, and the shop? It is but putting on our armor before we go out to battle."

Bragwell: "For my part, I think example is the whole of religion, and if the master of a family is orderly, and regular, and goes to church, he does everything which can be required of him, and no one has a right to call him to account for anything more."

Worthy: "Give me leave to say, Mr. Bragwell, that highly as I rate a good example, still, I must set a good principle above it. I know I must keep good order, indeed, for the sake of others; but I must keep a good conscience for my own sake. To God I owe secret piety. I must therefore pray to Him in private. To my family I owe a Christian example, and for that, among other reasons, I must not fail to go to church."

Bragwell: "You are talking, Mr. Worthy, as if I were an enemy to religion. Sir, I am no heathen. Sir, I am a Christian. I belong to the church; I go to church; I always drink prosperity to the church. You yourself, as strict as you are in never missing it twice a day, are not a warmer friend to the church than I am."

Worthy: "That is to say, you know its value as an institution; but you do not seem to know that a man may be very irreligious under the best religious institutions, and that even the most excellent of them are but means of being religious, and are no more religion itself than brick and mortar are prayers and thanksgivings. I shall never think, however high their profession and even however regular their attendance, that those men truly respect the church who bring home little of that religion which is taught in it into their own families or their own hearts, or who make the whole of Christianity to consist in a mere formal attendance there. Excuse me, Mr. Bragwell."

Bragwell: "Mr. Worthy, I am persuaded that religion is quite a proper thing for the poor, and I don't think that the multitude can ever be kept in order without it; and I am a sort of politician, you know. We must have bits, and bridles, and restraints for the vulgar."

Worthy: "Your opinion is very just, as far as it goes; but it does not go far enough, since it does not go to the root of the evil; for while you value yourself on the soundness of this principle as a politician, I wish you also to see the reason of it as a Christian. Depend upon it, if religion be good for the community at large, it is equally good for every family; and what is right for a family is equally right for each individual in it. You have, therefore, yourself brought the most unanswerable argument why you ought to be religious yourself, by asking how we shall keep others in order without religion. For, believe me, Mr. Bragwell, there is no particular clause to except you, in the gospel. There are no exceptions there in favor of any one class of men. The same restraints that are necessary for the people at large are equally necessary for men of every order, high and low, rich and poor, bond and free, learned and ignorant. If Jesus Christ died for no particular rank, class, or community, then there is no rank, class, or community, exempt from the obedience to His laws enjoined by the gospel. May I ask you, Mr. Bragwell, what is your reason for going to church?"

Bragwell: "Sir, I am shocked at your question. How can I avoid doing a thing so customary and so creditable? Not go to church, indeed! What do you take me for, Mr. Worthy? I am afraid you suspect me to be an atheist or a heathen, or of some religion or other that is not Christian."

Worthy: "If a foreigner were to hear how violently one set of Christians in this country often speak against another, how earnest would he suppose us all to be in religious matters, and how astonished to discover that many a man has perhaps little other proof to give of the sincerity of his own religion, except the violence with which he hates the religion of another party? It is not irreligion that such men hate, but the religion of the man, or the party, whom they are set against. Now hatred is certainly no part of the religion of the gospel. Well, you have told me why you go to church; now pray tell me, why do you confess there, on your bended knees, every Sunday, that 'you have erred and strayed from God's ways,' that 'there is no health in you,' that 'you have done what you ought not to do,' and that 'you are a miserable sinner'?"

Bragwell: "Because it is in the Common Prayer Book, to be sure—a book which I have heard you yourself say was written by wise and good men, the pillars of the Protestant church."

Worthy: "But have you no other reason?"

Bragwell: "No, I can't say I have."

Worthy: "When you repeat that excellent form of confession, do you really feel that you are a miserable sinner?"

Bragwell: "No, I can't say I do. But that is no objection to my repeating it, because it may suit the case of many who are so. I suppose the good doctors who drew it up intended that part for wicked people only, such as drunkards, and thieves, and murderers, for I imagine they could not well contrive to make the same prayer quite suit an honest man and a rogue; and so I suppose they thought it safer to make a good man repeat a prayer which suited a rogue, than to make a rogue repeat a prayer which suited a good man. And you know it is so customary for every body to repeat the general confession, that it can't hurt the credit of the most respectable persons, though every respectable person must know they have no particular concern in it, as they are not sinners."

Worthy: "Depend upon it, Mr. Bragwell, those good doctors you speak of were not quite of your opinion They really thought that those whom you call honest men, were grievous sinners in a certain sense, and that the best of us stand in need of making that humble confession. Mr. Bragwell, do you believe in the fall of Adam?"

Bragwell: "To be sure I do, and a sad thing for Adam it was. Why, it is in the Bible, is it not? It is one of the prettiest chapters in Genesis. Don't you believe it, Mr. Worthy?"

Worthy: "Yes, truly I do. But I don't believe it merely because I read it in Genesis, though I know, indeed, that I am bound to believe every part of the Word of God. But I have still an additional reason for believing in the fall of the first man."

Bragwell: "Have you, indeed? Now, I can't guess what that can be."

Worthy: "Why, my own observation of what is within myself teaches me to believe it. It is not only the third chapter of Genesis which convinces me of the truth of the fall, but also the sinful inclinations which I find in my own heart corresponding with it. This is one of those leading truths of Christianity of which I can never doubt a moment; first, because it is abundantly expressed or implied in Scripture; and next, because the consciousness of the evil nature I carry about with me confirms the doctrine beyond all doubt. Besides, is it not said in Scripture, that 'by one man sin entered into the world,' and that 'all we like sheep have gone astray,' that 'by one man's disobedience many were made sinners;' and so again in twenty more places that I could tell you of?"

Bragwell: "Well, I never thought of this. But is not this a very melancholy sort of doctrine, Mr. Worthy?"

Worthy: "It is melancholy, indeed, if we stop here. But while we are deploring this sad truth, let us take comfort from another, that 'as in Adam all die, even so in Christ shall all be made alive.'"

Bragwell: "Yes, I remember I thought those very fine words, when I heard them said over my poor father's grave. But as it was in the burial of the dead, I did not think of taking it to myself, for I was then young and hearty, and in little danger of dying, and I have been so busy ever since that I have hardly had time to think of it."

Worthy: "And yet the service pronounced at the burial of all who die is a solemn admonition to all who live. It is there said, as indeed the Scripture says also, 'I am the resurrection, and the life; whosoever believeth in Me shall never die, but I will raise him up at the last day.' Now do you think you believe in Christ, Mr. Brag-well?"

Bragwell: "To be sure I do. Why, you are always fancying me an atheist."

Worthy: "In order to believe in Christ, we must believe first in our own guilt and our own unworthiness; and when we do this, we shall see the need of a Saviour, and not till then."

Bragwell: "Why, all this is a new way of talking. I can't say I ever meddled with such subjects before in my life. But now, what do you advise a man to do upon your plan of religion?"

Worthy: "Why, all this leads me back to the ground from which we set out. I mean the duty of prayer; for if we believe that we have an evil nature within us, and that we stand in need of God's grace to help us, and a Saviour to redeem us, we shall be led of course to pray for what we so much need; and without this conviction we shall not be led to pray."

Bragwell: "Well, but don't you think, Mr. Worthy, that you good folks who make so much of prayer have lower notions than we have of the wisdom of the Almighty? You think He wants to be informed of the things you tell Him; whereas, I take it for granted that He knows them already, and that, being so good as He is, He will give me everything He sees fit to give me, without my asking it."

Worthy: "God, indeed, who knows all things, knows what we want before we ask Him; but still, has He not said, that 'with prayer and supplication we must make known our requests unto Him'? Prayer is the way in which God hath said that His favor must be sought. It is the channel through which He has declared it is His sovereign will and pleasure that His blessings should be conveyed to us. What ascends up in prayer descends again to us in blessings. It is like the rain which just now fell, and which had been drawn up from the ground in vapors to the clouds before it descended from them to the earth in that refreshing shower. Besides, prayer has a good effect on our minds; it tends to excite a right disposition towards God in us, and to keep up a constant sense of our dependence. But above all, it is the way to get the good things we want. 'Ask,' says the Scripture, 'and ye shall receive.'"

Bragwell: "Now this is the very thing which I was going to deny. For the truth is, men do not always get what they ask. I believe, if I could get a good crop for asking it, I should pray more often than I do."

Worthy: "Sometimes, Mr. Bragwell, men 'ask and receive not, because they ask amiss,' they ask, that they 'may consume it on their lusts.' They ask worldly blessings, perhaps, when they should ask spiritual ones. Now the latter, which are the good things I spoke of, are always granted to those who pray to God for them, though the former are not. I have observed, in the case of some worldly things I have sought for, that the grant of my prayer would have caused the misery of my life, so that God equally consults our good in what He withholds, and in what He bestows."

Bragwell: "And yet you continue to pray on, I suppose."

Worthy: "Certainly; but then I try to mend as to the object of my prayers. I pray for God's blessing and favor, which is better than riches."

Bragwell: "You seem very earnest on this subject."

Worthy: "To cut the matter short, I ask, then, whether prayer is not positively commanded in the gospel? When this is the case, we can never dispute about the necessity or the duty of a thing, as we may when there is no such command. Here, however, let me just add also, that a man's prayers may be turned to no small use in the way of discovering to him whatever is amiss in his life."

Bragwell: "How so, Mr. Worthy?"

Worthy: "Why, suppose now, you were to try yourself by turning into the shape of a prayer every practice in which you allow yourself. For instance, let the prayer in the morning be a sort of preparation for the deeds of the day, and the prayer at night a sort of review of those deeds. You, Mr. Bragwell, I suspect, are a little inclined to covetousness; excuse me sir. Now suppose, after you have been during a whole day a little too eager to get rich, suppose, I say, you were to try how it would sound to beg of God at night, on your knees, to give you still more money, though you have already so much that you know not what to do with it. Suppose you were to pray in the morning, 'O Lord, give me more riches, though those I have are a snare and a temptation to me,' and ask Him in the same solemn manner to bless all the grasping means you intend to make use of in the day to add to your substance."

Bragwell: "Mr. Worthy, I have no patience with you for thinking I could be so wicked."

Worthy: "Hear me out, Mr. Bragwell. You turned your good nephew, Tom Broad, out-of doors, you know; you admitted to me it was an act of injustice. Now suppose, on the morning of your doing so, you had begged of God in a solemn act of prayer, to prosper the deed of cruelty and oppression which you intended to commit that day. I see you are shocked at the thought of such a prayer. Well, then, would not hearty prayer have kept you from committing that wicked action?

"In short, what a life must that be, no act of which you dare beg God to prosper and bless. If once you can bring yourself to believe that it is your bounden duty to pray for God's blessings on your day's work, you will certainly grow careful about passing such a day as you may safely ask His blessing upon. The remark may be carried to sports, diversions, and company. A man who once takes up the serious use of prayer will soon find himself obliged to abstain from such diversions, occupations, and societies as he cannot reasonably desire that God will bless to him, and thus he will see himself compelled to leave off either the practice or the prayer. Now, Mr. Bragwell, I need not ask you which of the two he that is a real Christian will give up, sinning or praying."

Mr. Bragwell began to feel that he had not the best of the argument, and was afraid he was making no great figure in the eyes of his friend. However, he was relieved from the difficulty into which the necessity of making some answer must have brought him by finding they had come to the end of their little journey, and he never beheld the bunch of grapes that decorated the sign of the Golden Lion with more real satisfaction.

I refer my readers for the transactions at the Golden Lion, and for the sad adventures that afterwards befell Mr. Bragwell's family, to the fifth part of the history of the Two Wealthy Farmers.

Part 5

THE GOLDEN LION

Mr. Bragwell and Mr. Worthy stopped at the Golden Lion. It was market-day; the inn, the yard, and the town, were all alive. Mr. Bragwell was quite in his element. Money, company, and good cheer, always set his spirits afloat. He felt himself the principal man in the scene. He had three great objects in view: the sale of his land, letting Mr. Worthy see how much he was looked up to by so many substantial people, and showing these people what a wise man his most intimate friend Mr. Worthy was. It was his way to try to borrow a little credit from every person and everything he was connected with, and by that credit to advance his interest and increase his wealth.

The farmers met in a large room, and while they were transacting their various concerns those whose pursuits were the same naturally herded together. The tanners were drawn to one corner by the common interest that they took in bark and hides. A useful debate was carrying on at another little table, whether the practice of sowing wheat or of planting it were most profitable. Another set were disputing whether horses or oxen were best for plows. Those who were concerned in canals sought the company of other canal owners, while some, who were interested in the new bill for enclosures, wisely looked out for such as know most about waste lands.

Mr. Worthy was pleased with all these subjects, and picked up something useful on each. It was a saying of his that most men understood some one thing, and that he who was wise would try to learn from every man something on the subject he best knew, but Mr. Worthy made a further use of the whole. "What a pity it is," said he, "that Christians are not as desirous to turn their time to good account as men of business are. When shall we see religious persons as anxious to derive profit from the experience of others as these farmers? When shall we see them as eager to turn their time to good account? While I approve these men for not being 'slothful in business,' let me improve the hint, by being also 'fervent in spirit'."

SHOWING HOW MUCH WISER THE CHILDREN OF THIS GENERATION ARE THAN THE CHILDREN OF LIGHT

When the hurry was a little over, Mr. Bragwell took a turn on the Bowling-green. Mr. Worthy followed him to ask why the sale of the estate was not brought forward. "Let the auctioneer proceed to business," said he; "the company will be glad to get home by daylight. I speak mostly with a view to others, for I do not think of being a purchaser myself."

"I know it," said Bragwell, "or I would not be such a fool as to let the cat out of the bag. But is it really possible," proceeded he with a smile of contempt, "that you should think I will sell my estate before dinner. Mr. Worthy, you are a clever man at books, and such things, and perhaps can make out an account on paper in a handsomer manner than I can, but I never found much was to be got by fine writing. As to figures, I can carry enough of them in my head to add, divide, and multiply more money than your learning will ever give you the fingering of. You may beat me at a book, but you are a very child at a bargain. Sell my land before dinner, indeed!"

Mr. Worthy was puzzled to guess how a man was to show more wisdom by selling a piece of ground at one hour than at another, and desired an explanation. Bragwell felt rather more contempt for his understanding than he had ever done before.

"Look here, Mr. Worthy," said he, "I do not know that knowledge is of any use to a man unless he has sense enough to turn it to account. Men are my books, Mr. Worthy, and it is by reading, spelling, and putting them together to good purpose that I have got up in the world. I shall give you a proof of this today. These farmers have most of them come to the Lion with a view of purchasing this bit of land of mine, if they should like the bargain. Now, as you know a thing can't be any great bargain both to the buyer and the seller too, to them and to me, it becomes me, as a man of sense, who has the good of his family at heart, to secure the bargain to myself. I would not cheat any man, sir, but I think it fair enough to turn his weakness to my own advantage. There is no law against that, you know; and this is the use of one man's having more sense than another.

"So, whenever I have a bit of land to sell, I always give a handsome dinner, with plenty of punch and strong beer. We fill up the morning with other business, and I carefully keep back any talk about the purchase till we have dined. At dinner we have, of course, a bit of politics. This puts most of us into an angry mood, and you know anger is thirsty. Besides, 'church and king' naturally brings on a good many other toasts. Now, as I am master of the feast, you know, it would be shabby in me to save my liquor, so I push about the glass one way, and the tankard the other, till all my company are as merry as kings. Every man is delighted to see what a fine hearty fellow he has to deal with, and Mr. Bragwell receives a thousand compliments.

"By this time they have gained as much in good humor as they have lost in sober judgment, and this is the proper moment for setting the auctioneer to work; and this I commonly do to such good purpose, that I go home with my purse a score or two of pounds heavier than if they had not been warmed by their dinner. In the morning men are cool and suspicious, and have all their wits about them; but a cheerful glass cures all distrust. And, what is more, I add to my credit as well as my pocket, and get more praise for my dinner than blame for my bargain."

Mr. Worthy was struck with the absurd vanity that could tempt a man to own himself guilty of an unfair action for the sake of showing his wisdom. He was beginning to express his disapproval when they were told dinner was on the table. They went in, and were soon seated. All was mirth and good cheer. Everyone agreed that no one gave such hearty dinners as Mr. Bragwell. Nothing was pitiful where he was master of the feast. Bragwell, who looked with pleasure on the excellent dinner before him, and enjoyed the good account to which he should turn it, heard their praises with delight, and cast an eye on Worthy, as much as to say, "Who is the wise man now?" Having a mind, for his own credit, to make his friend talk, he turned to him, saying, "Mr. Worthy, I believe no people in the world enjoy life more than men of our class. We have money and power; we live on the fat of the land, and have as good a right to gentility as the best."

"As to gentility, Mr. Bragwell," replied Worthy, "I am not sure that this is among the wisest of our pretensions; but I will say that ours is a creditable and respectable business. In ancient times, farming was the employment of princes and patriarchs, and now-a-days, an honest, humane, sensible English farmer, I will be bold to say, is not only a very useful but an honorable character.

"But then, he must not merely think of enjoying life, as you call it, but he must think of living up to the great ends for which he was sent into the world. A wealthy farmer not only has it in his power to live well, but to do much good. He is not only the father of his own family, but of his workmen, his dependents, and the poor at large, especially in these hard times. He has it in his power to raise into credit all the parish offices that have fallen into disrepute, by getting into bad hands, and he can convert what have been falsely thought mean offices into very important ones, by his just and Christian-like manner of filling them.

"An upright juryman, a conscientious constable, a human overseer, an independent elector, an active superintendent of a work-house, a just arbitrator in public disputes, a kind counselor in private troubles—such a one, I say, fills a station in society no less necessary, and, as far as it reaches, scarcely less important than that of a magistrate, a sheriff of a county, or even a member of Parliament. That can never be a slight or a degrading office on which the happiness of a whole parish may depend."

Bragwell, who thought the good sense of his friend reflected credit on himself, encouraged Worthy to go on, but he did it in his own vain way. "Aye, very true, Mr. Worthy," said he, "you are right. A leading man in our class ought to be looked up to as an example, as you say, in order to which he

The Two Wealthy Farmers

should do things handsomely and liberally, and not grudge himself or his friends anything," casting an eye of complacency on the good dinner he had provided.

"True," replied Mr. Worthy, "he should be an example of simplicity, sobriety, and plainness of manners. But he will do well not to affect a frivolous gentility, which will sit but clumsily upon him. If he has no money, let him spend prudently, lay up moderately for his children, and give liberally to the poor; but let him rather seek to dignify his own station by his virtues, than to get above it by his vanity. If he acts thus, then, as long as this country lasts, a farmer of England will be looked upon as one of its most valuable members; nay, more, by this conduct he may contribute to make England last the longer. The riches of the farmer, corn and cattle, are the true riches of a nation; but let him remember, that though corn and cattle enrich a country, nothing but justice, integrity, and religion, can preserve it."

Young Wilson, the worthy grazier whom Miss Bragwell had turned off because he did not understand French dances, thanked Mr. Worthy for what he had said, and hoped that he should be the better for it as long as he lived, and desired his leave to be better acquainted. Most of the others declared they had never heard a finer speech, and then, as usual, proceeded to show the good effect it had on them, by loose conversation, hard drinking, and whatever could counteract all that Mr. Worthy had said.

Mr. Worthy was much concerned to hear Mr. Bragwell, after dinner, whisper to the waiter to put less and less water into every fresh bowl of punch. This was his way; if the time they had to sit was long, then the punch was to be weaker, as he saw no good in wasting money to make it stronger than the time required. But if time pressed, then the strength was to be increased in due proportion, as a small quantity must then intoxicate them as much in a short time as would be required of a greater quantity had the time been longer. This was one of Mr. Bragwell's nice calculations, and this was the sort of skill on which he so much valued himself.

At length the guests were properly primed for business, just in that convenient stage of intoxication that makes men warm and rash, yet keeps short of that absolute drunkenness which disqualifies for business. The auctioneer set to work. All were bidders, and, if possible, all would have been purchasers, so happily had the feast and the punch operated. They bid on with still increasing spirit, till they had got so much above the value of the land that Bragwell, with a wink and a whisper, said, "Who would sell his land fasting, eh, Worthy?" At length the estate was knocked down, at a price very far above its worth.

As soon as it was sold, Bragwell again said softly to Worthy, "Five from fifty, and there remain forty-five. The dinner and drink won't cost me five pounds, and I have got fifty more than the land was worth. Spend a shilling to gain a pound; this is what I call practical arithmetic, Mr. Worthy."

Mr. Worthy was glad to get out of this scene; and seeing that his friend was quite sober, he resolved, as they rode home, to deal plainly with him. Bragwell had found out, among his calculations, that there were some sins that could only be committed by a prudent man one at a time. For instance, he knew that a man could not well get rich and get drunk at the same moment, so that he used to practice one first, and the other after; but he had found out that some vices made very good company together; thus, while he had watched himself in drinking lest he should become as unfit to sell as his guests were to buy, he had indulged without measure in the good dinner he had provided. Mr. Worthy, I say, seeing him able to bear reason, rebuked him for this day's proceedings with some severity. Bragwell bore his reproof with that sort of patience that arises from an opinion of one's own wisdom, and a recent flush of prosperity. He behaved with that gay good-humor which grows out of vanity and good luck.

"You are too scrupulous, Mr. Worthy," said he; "I have done nothing discreditable. These men came with their eyes open. There is no compulsion used. They are free to bid, or to let it alone. I make them welcome, and I shall not be thought a bit the worse of by them tomorrow, when they are sober. Others do it besides me, and I shall never be ashamed of anything as long as I have custom on my side."

Worthy: "I am sorry, Mr. Bragwell, to hear you support such practices by such arguments. There is not, perhaps, a more dangerous snare to the souls of men than is to be found in that word custom. It is a word invented to reconcile corruption with credit, and sin with safety. But no custom, no fashion, no combination of men to set up a false standard, can ever make a wrong action right. That a thing is often done, is so far from a proof of its being right, that it is the very reason which will set a thinking man to inquire if it be not really wrong, lest he should be following a 'multitude to do evil.'

"Right 'is right, though only one man in a thousand pursue it; and wrong will be forever wrong, though it be the allowed practice of the other nine hundred and ninety-nine.' If this shameful custom is really common, which I can hardly believe, that is a fresh reason why a conscientious man should set his face against it. And I must go so far as to say—you will excuse me, Mr. Bragwell—that I see no great difference in the eye of conscience, whatever there may be in the eye of law, between your making a man first lose his reason, and then getting fifty guineas out of his pocket because he has lost it, and your picking the fifty guineas out of his pocket if you had met him dead drunk on his way home to-night. Nay, he who meets a man already drunk and robs him commits but one sin, while he who makes him drunk first, that he may rob him afterwards, commits two."

Bragwell gravely replied, "Mr. Worthy, while I have the practice of people of credit to support me, and the law of the land to protect me, I see no reason to be ashamed of anything I do."

"Mr. Bragwell," answered Worthy, "a truly honest man is not always looking sharp about him, to see how far custom and the law will bear him out; if he be honest on principle, he will consult the law of his conscience, and if he be a Christian, he will consult the written law of God."

Notwithstanding this rebuff, Mr. Bragwell got home in high spirits, for no arguments could hinder him from feeling that he had the fifty guineas in his purse. As soon as he came in, he gaily threw the money he had received on the table, and desired his wife to lock it up. Instead of receiving it with her usual satisfaction, she burst into a violent fit of anger, and threw it back to him.

"You may keep your cash yourself," said she. "It is all over; we want no more money. You are a ruined man. A wicked creature; scraping and working as we have done for her!"

Bragwell trembled, but dared not ask what he dreaded to hear. His wife spared him the trouble by crying out, as soon as her rage permitted, "Polly is gone off!"

Poor Bragwell's heart sunk within him; he grew sick and giddy; and as his wife's rage swallowed up her grief, so, in his grief, he almost forgot his anger. The purse fell from his hand and he cast a look of anguish upon it, finding, for the first time, that money could not relieve his misery.

Mr. Worthy, who, though much concerned, was less discomposed, now called to mind that the young lady had not returned with her mother and sister the night before, and he begged Mrs. Bragwell to explain this sad story. She, instead of soothing her husband, fell to reproaching him.

"It is all your fault," said she; "you were a fool for your pains. If I had had my way, the girls never would have kept company with any but men of substance, and then they could not have been ruined."

"Mrs. Bragwell," said Mr. Worthy, "if she has chosen a bad man, it would be still a misfortune, even though he had been rich."

"O, that would alter the case," said she. "A fat sorrow is better than a lean one. But to marry a beggar! There is no sin like that."

Here Miss Betsy, who stood sullenly by, put in a word, and said her sister, however, had not disgraced herself by having married a farmer or a tradesman; she had, at least, made choice of a gentleman.

"What marriage? What gentleman?" cried the afflicted father. "Tell me the worst."

He was now informed that his darling daughter had gone off with a strolling actor, who had been acting in the neighboring villages lately. Miss Betsy again put in, saying he was no stroller, but a gentleman in disguise, who only acted for his own diversion.

"Does he so?" said the now furious Bragwell, "then he shall be transported for mine."

At this moment a letter was brought him from his new son-in-law, who desired his leave to wait upon him and implore his forgiveness. He said he had been a shopkeeper for a tailor, but thinking his person and talents ought not to be thrown away upon trade, and being also low on money, he had taken to the stage with a view of making his fortune; that he had married Miss Bragwell entirely for love, and was sorry to mention so small a thing as money, which he despised, but that his bills were pressing; his landlord, to whom he was in debt, having been so vulgar as to threaten to send him to prison. He ended with saying:

"I have been obliged to shock your daughter's delicacy by confessing my real name. I believe I owe part of my success with her to my having assumed that of Augustus Frederick Theodosius. She is inconsolable at this confession, which, as you are now my father, I must also make to you, and subscribe myself, with many blushes, by the vulgar name of your dutiful son,

Timothy Incle"

"O," cried the afflicted father, as he tore the letter in a rage, "Miss Bragwell married to a strolling actor! How shall I bear it?"

"Why, I would not bear it at all," cried the enraged mother, "I would never see her, I would never forgive her, I would let her starve at one corner of the barn while that rascal was ranting away at the other."

"Nay," said Miss Betsy, "if he is only a store-keeper, and if his name be really Timothy Incle, I would never forgive her neither. But who would have thought it by his looks, and by his monstrous refined behavior? No, he never can have so vulgar a name."

"Come, come," said Mr. Worthy, "were he really an honest tailor, I should think there was no other harm done, except the disobedience of the thing. Mr. Bragwell, this is no time to blame you, or hardly to reason with you; I feel for you sincerely. I ought not, perhaps, just at present, to reproach you for the mistaken manner in which you have brought up your daughters, as your error has brought its punishment along with it. You now see, because you now feel the evil of a false education. It has ruined your daughter; your whole plan unavoidably led to some such end. The large sums you spent to qualify them, as you thought, for a high station, could do them nothing but harm, while your habits of life properly confined them to company of a lower class. While they were better dressed than the daughters of the upper class, they were worse taught, as to real knowledge, than the daughters of your plowmen. Their vanity has been raised by excessive flattery. Every evil temper has been fostered by indulgence.

88

Their pride has never been controlled; their self-will has never been subdued. Their idleness has laid them open to every temptation, and their abundance has enabled them to gratify every desire. Their time, that precious talent, has been entirely wasted. Everything they have been taught to do is of no use, while they are utterly unacquainted with all that they ought to have known. I deplore Miss Polly's false step. That she should have married a runaway shopkeeper-turned-actor, I truly lament. But, for what better husband was she qualified? For the wife of a farmer, she was too idle; for the wife of a tradesman, she was too expensive; for the wife of a gentleman, she was too ignorant. You yourself were most to blame. You expected her to act wisely, though you never taught her that 'fear of God which is the beginning of wisdom.' I owe it to you as a friend, and to myself as a Christian, to declare that your practices in the common transactions of life, as well as your present misfortune, are almost the natural consequences of those false principles which I protested against when you were at my house."

Mrs. Bragwell attempted several times to interrupt Mr. Worthy, but her husband would not permit it. He felt the force of all his friend said, and encouraged him to proceed. Mr. Worthy thus went on:

"It grieves me to say how much your own indiscretion has contributed even to bring on your present misfortune. You gave your consent to this very company of actors, though you knew they were acting in defiance of the laws of the land, to say no worse. They go from town to town, and from barn to barn, stripping the poor of their money, the young of their innocence, and all of their time. Do you remember with how much pride you told me that you had bespoke the 'Bold Stroke for a Wife,' for the benefit of this very Mr. Frederick Theodosius? To this destructive language you not only carried your own family, but wasted I know not how much money in treating your workmen's wives and children, in these hard times too, when they have scarcely bread to eat, or a shoe on their feet. And all this only that you might have the absurd pleasure of seeing those flattering words, 'By desire of Mr. Bragwell,' stuck up in print at the public-house, on the blacksmith's shed, at the turnpike-gate, and on the barn-door."

Mr. Bragwell acknowledged that his friend's rebuke was but too just, and he looked so very contrite as to raise the pity of Mr. Worthy, who, in a mild voice, thus went on:

"What I have said is not so much to reproach you with the ruin of one daughter, as from a desire to save the other. Let Miss Betsy go home with me. I do not undertake to be her jailer, but I will be her friend. She will find in my daughters kind companions, and in my wife a prudent guide. I know she will dislike us at first, but I do not despair in time of convincing her that a sober, humble, useful, pious life is as necessary to make us happy on earth as it is to fit us for heaven."

Poor Miss Betsy, though she declared it would be frightful dull, and monstrous vulgar, and dismal melancholy, yet she was so terrified at the discontent and grumbling which she would have to endure at home that she sullenly consented. She had none of that tenderness which led her to wish to stay and soothe and comfort her afflicted father. All she thought about was to get out of the way of her mother's ill humor, and to carry so much finery with her as to fill the Misses Worthy with envy and respect. Poor girl, she did not know that envy was a feeling they never indulge, and that fine clothes was the last thing to draw their respect.

Mr. Worthy took her home next day. When they reached his house, they found there young Wilson, Miss Betsy's old admirer. She was much pleased at this, and resolved to treat him well. But her good or ill treatment now signified but little. This young grazier reverenced Mr. Worthy's character, and ever since he had met him at the Lion, had been thinking what a happiness it would be to marry a young woman brought up by such a father. He had heard much of the modesty and discretion of both the daughters, but his inclination now determined him in favor of the elder.

Mr. Worthy, who knew him to be a young man of good sense and sound principles, allowed him to become a visitor at his house, but deferred his consent to the marriage till he knew him more thoroughly. Mr. Wilson, from what he saw of the domestic piety of this family, improved daily both in the knowledge and practice of religion, and Mr. Worthy soon formed him into a most valuable character.

During this time Miss Bragwell's hopes had revived, but though she appeared in a new dress almost every day, she had the mortification of being beheld with great indifference by one whom she had always secretly liked. Mr. Wilson married before her face a girl who was greatly her inferior in fortune, person, and appearance, but who was humble, frugal, meek, and pious. Miss Bragwell now strongly felt the truth of what Mr. Wilson had once told her, that a woman might make an excellent partner for a dance who would make a very bad one for life.

Hitherto Mr. Bragwell and his daughters had only learned to regret their folly and vanity, as it had produced them mortification in this life. Whether they were ever brought to a more serious sense of their errors, may be seen in a future part of this history.

Part 6

GOOD RESOLUTIONS

Mr. Bragwell was so much afflicted at the disgraceful marriage of his daughter, who ran off with Timothy Incle the actor, that he never fully recovered his spirits. His cheerfulness, which had arisen from a high opinion of himself, had been confirmed by a constant flow of uninterrupted success, and that is a sort of cheerfulness which is very liable to be impaired, because it lies at the mercy of every accident and cross event in life. But though his pride was now disappointed, his misfortunes had not taught him any humility, because he had not discovered that they were caused by his own fault; nor had he acquired any patience or submission, because he had not learned that all afflictions come from the hand of God to awaken us to a deep sense of our sins, and to draw off our hearts from the perishing vanities of this life.

Besides, Mr. Bragwell was one of those people who, even if they would be thought to bear with tolerable submission such trials as appear to be sent more immediately from Providence, yet think they have a right to rebel at every misfortune which befalls them through the fault of a fellow-creature, as if our fellow-creatures were not the agents and instruments by which Providence often sees fit to try or to punish us.

His imprudent daughter, Bragwell would not be brought to see or forgive, nor was the degrading name of Mrs. Incle ever allowed to be pronounced in his hearing. He had loved her with an excessive and undue affection, and while she gratified his vanity by her beauty and finery, he deemed her faults of little consequence; but when she disappointed his ambition by a disgraceful marriage, all his natural affection only served to increase his resentment. Yet, though he regretted her crime less than his own mortifications, he never ceased in secret to lament her loss.

She soon found out that she was undone, and wrote in a strain of bitter repentance to ask his forgiveness. She admitted that her husband, whom she had supposed to be a man of fashion in disguise, was a low person in distressed circumstances. She implored that her father, though he refused to give her husband that fortune for which alone it was now too plain he had married her, would at least allow her some subsistence, for that Mr. Incle was much in debt, and she feared in danger of a jail.

The father's heart was half melted at this account, and his affection was for a time awakened. But Mrs. Bragwell opposed his sending her any assistance. She always made it a point of duty never to forgive, for she said it only encouraged those who had done wrong once to do worse next time. For her part, she had never yet been guilty of so mean and pitiful a weakness as to forgive anyone, for to pardon an injury always showed either want of spirit to feel it, or want of power to resent it. She was resolved she would never squander the money for which she had worked early and late on a baggage who had thrown herself away on a beggar, while she had a daughter single who might yet raise her family by a great match.

I am sorry to say that Mrs. Bragwell's anger was not owing to the undutifulness of the daughter, or the worthlessness of the husband; poverty was, in her eyes, the grand crime. The doctrine of forgiveness, as a religious principle, made no more a part of Mr. Bragwell's system than of his wife's, but in natural feeling, particularly for this offending daughter, he much exceeded her.

In a few months, the youngest Miss Bragwell desired permission to return home from Mrs. Worthy's. She had, indeed, only consented to go there as a less evil of the two, than staying in her father's house after her sister's elopement. But the sobriety and simplicity of Mr. Worthy's family were irksome to her. Habits of vanity and idleness had become so rooted in her mind that any degree of restraint was a burden, and though she was outwardly civil, it was easy to see that she longed to get away. She resolved, however, to profit by her sister's faults, and made her parents easy, by assuring them she never would throw herself away on a man who was worth nothing. Encouraged by these promises, which were all that her parents thought they could in reason expect, her father allowed her to come home.

Mr. Worthy, who accompanied her, found Mr. Bragwell gloomy and dejected. As his house was no longer a scene of vanity and festivity, Mr. Bragwell tried to make himself and his friend believe that he was grown religious, whereas he was only become discontented As he had always fancied that piety was melancholy, gloomy thing, and as he felt his own mind really gloomy, he was willing to think that he was growing pious.

He had, indeed, gone more constantly to church, and had taken less pleasure in feasting and cards, and now and then read a chapter in the Bible, but all this was because his spirits were low, and not because his heart was changed. The outward actions were more regular, but the inward man was the same. The forms of religion were resorted to as a painful duty, but this only added to his misery, while he was utterly ignorant of its spirit and its power. He still, however, reserved religion as a loathsome medicine, to which he feared he must have recourse at last, and of which he even now considered every abstinence from pleasure, or every exercise of piety, as a bitter dose.

His health also was impaired, so that his friend found him in a pitiable state, neither able to receive pleasure from the world which he so dearly loved, nor from religion which he so greatly feared. He expected to have been much commended by Worthy for the change in his way of life; but Worthy, who saw that the change was only owing to the loss of animal spirits, and to the casual absence of temptation, was cautious of flattering him too much.

"I thought, Mr. Worthy," said he, "to have received more comfort from you. I was told, too, that religion was full of comfort, but I do not much find it."

"You were told the truth," replied Worthy. "Religion is full of comfort, but you must first be brought into a state fit to receive it before it can become so; you must be brought to a deep and humbling sense of sin. To give you comfort while you are puffed up with high thoughts of yourself would be to give you a strong stimulant in a high fever. Religion keeps back her cures till the patient is lowered and emptied—emptied of self, Mr. Bragwell. If you had a wound, it must be examined and cleansed, yes, and probed too, before it would be safe to put on a healing bandage. Curing it to the outward eye, while it was corrupt at bottom, would only bring on mortification, and you would be a dead man while you trusted that the bandage was curing you. You must be indeed a Christian before you can be entitled to the comforts of Christianity."

"I am a Christian," said Bragwell, "many of my friends are Christians, but I do not see that it has done us much good."

"Christianity itself," answered Mr. Worthy, "cannot make us good unless it be applied to our hearts. Christian privileges will not make us Christians unless we make use of them. On that shelf

I see stands your medicine. The doctor orders you to take it. Have you taken it?"

"Yes," replied Bragwell.

"Are you the better for it?" said Worthy.

"I think I am," he replied.

"But," added Worthy, "are you the better because the doctor has ordered it merely, or because you have also taken it?"

"What a foolish question!" cried Bragwell. "Why, to be sure the doctor might be the best doctor, and his medicine the best medicine in the world, but if it stood forever on the shelf, I could not expect to be cured by it. My doctor is not a fraud. He does not pretend to cure by a charm. The medicine is good, and as it suits my case, though it is bitter, I take it."

"You have now," said Worthy, "explained the reason why religion does so little good in this world. It is not a fraud, it does not work by a charm, but offers to cure your worst corruptions by wholesome, though sometimes bitter prescriptions. But you will not take them; you will not apply to God with the same earnest desire to be healed with which you apply to your doctor; you will not confess your sins to the one as honestly as you tell your symptoms to the other, nor read your Bible with the same faith and submission with which you take your medicine. In reading it, however, you must take care not to apply to yourself the comforts that are not suited to your case. You must, by the grace of God, be brought into a condition to be entitled to the promises, before you can expect the comfort of them. Conviction is not conversion; that worldly discontent which is the effect of worldly disappointment, is not that 'godly sorrow which worketh repentance.' Besides, while you have been pursuing all the gratifications of the world, do not complain that you have not all the comforts of religion too. Could you live in the full enjoyment of both, the Bible would not be true."

Bragwell now seemed resolved to set about the matter in earnest, but he resolved in his own strength; and unluckily, the very day Mr. Worthy took leave, there happened to be a grand ball at the next town, on account of the assizes. An assize-ball is a scene to which gentlemen and ladies periodically resort to celebrate the crimes and calamities of their fellow-creatures by dancing and music, and to divert themselves with feasting and drinking, while unhappy wretches are receiving sentence of death.

To this ball Miss Bragwell went, dressed out with a double portion of finery—pouring out on her head, in addition to her own ornaments, the whole bandbox of feathers, beads, and flowers her sister had left behind her.

While she was at the ball her father formed many plans of religious reformation. He talked of lessening his business, that he might have more leisure for devotion, though not just now while the markets were so high; and then he began to think of sending a handsome subscription to the hospital, though, on second thought, he concluded he need not be in a hurry, but leave it in his will. But to give, and repent, and reform, were three things he was bent upon.

But when his daughter came home at night, so happy and so fine, and telling how she had danced with Squire Squeeze the great corn-contractor, and how many fine things he had said to her, Mr. Bragwell felt the old spirit of the world return in its full force. A marriage with Mr. Dashall Squeeze, the contractor, was beyond his hopes, for Mr. Squeeze was supposed from a very low beginning to have got rich during the war. As for Mr. Squeeze, he had picked up as much of the history of his partner between the dances as he desired; he was convinced there would be no money wanting, for Miss Bragwell, who was now looked on as an only child, must needs be a great fortune, and he was too much used to advantageous contracts to let this slip. As he was gaudily dressed, and possessed all the arts of vulgar flattery, Miss Bragwell eagerly caught at his proposal to wait on her father next day.

Squeeze was quite a man after Bragwell's own heart, a genius at getting money, a fine, dashing fellow at spending it. He told his wife that this was the very sort of man for his daughter, for he got money like a Jew, and spent it like a prince; but whether it was fairly got, or wisely spent, he was too much a man of the world to inquire.

Mrs. Bragwell was not so run away with by appearances, but she desired her husband to be careful and make himself quite sure that it was the right Mr. Squeeze, and no imposter. But being assured that Betsy would certainly keep her carriage, she never gave herself one thought with what sort of a man she was to ride in it. To have one of her daughters drive in her own coach, filled up all her ideas of human happiness. The marriage was celebrated with great splendor, and Mr. and Mrs. Squeeze set off for London, where they had taken a house.

Mr. Bragwell now tried to forget that he had any other daughter, and if some thoughts of the resolutions he had made of entering on a more religious course would sometimes force themselves upon him, they were put off, like the repentance of Felix, to a more "convenient season." And finding he was likely to have a grandchild, he became more worldly and ambitious than ever, thinking this a just pretense for adding house to house, and field to field; and there is no stratagem by which men more fatally deceive themselves than when they make even unborn children a pretense for that plunder, or that hoarding, of which their own covetousness is the true motive.

Whenever he ventured to write to Mr. Worthy about the wealth, the gaiety, and the grandeur of Mr. and Mrs. Squeeze, that faithful friend honestly reminded him of the vanity and uncertainty of worldly greatness, and the error he had been guilty of in marrying his daughter before he had taken time to inquire into the real character of the man, saying, that he could not help foreboding that the happiness of a match made at a ball might have an untimely end.

Notwithstanding Mr. and Mrs. Bragwell had paid down a larger fortune than was prudent, for fear Mr. Squeeze should fly off, yet he was surprised to receive very soon a pressing letter from him, desiring him to advance a considerable sum, as he had the offer of an advantageous purchase which he must lose for want of money.

Bragwell was staggered, and refused to comply, but his wife told him he must not be shabby to such a gentleman as Squire Squeeze, for that she heard on all sides such accounts of their grandeur, their feasts, their carriages, and their liveries, that she and her husband ought even to deny themselves comforts to oblige such a generous son, who did all this in honor of their daughter. Besides, if he did not send the money soon, they might be obliged to sell their coach, and then she should never be able to show her face again.

At length Mr. Bragwell lent him the money on his bond; he knew Squeeze's income was large, for he had carefully inquired into this particular, and for the rest he took his word. Mrs. Squeeze also got great presents from her mother, by representing to her how expensively they were forced to live to keep up their credit, and what honor she was conferring on the family of the Bragwells by spending their money in such grand company. Among many other letters she wrote her the following:

"To Mrs. Bragwell:

"You can't imagine, dear mother, how charmingly we live—I lie abed almost all day, and am up all night; but it is never dark for all that, for we burn such numbers of candles all at once, that the sun would be of no use at all in London. Then I am so happy, for we are never quiet a moment, Sundays or working days; nay, I should not know which was which, only that we have most pleasure on the Sunday, because it is the only day in which people have nothing to do but divert themselves. Then the great folks are all so kind, and so good, that they have not a bit of pride, for they will come and eat and drink, and win my money just as if I was their equal; and if I have got but a cold, they are so very unhappy that they send to know how I do; and though I suppose they can't rest till the servant has told them, yet they are so polite, that if I have been dying they seem to have forgot it next time we meet, and not to know but they have seen me the day before. Oh, they are true friends, and forever smiling, and so fond of one another that they like to meet and enjoy one another's company by hundreds, and always think the more the merrier.

"Your dutiful daughter,
Betsy Squeeze"

The style of her letters, however, altered in a few months. She said that, though things went on gayer and grander than ever, yet she hardly ever saw her husband, except her house was full of company, and cards or dancing were going on; that he was often so busy he could not come home all night; that he always borrowed the money her mother sent her when he was going out on his nightly business; and that the last time she had asked him for money, he cursed, and swore, and bade her apply to the old farmer and his rib, who were made of money. This letter Mrs. Bragwell concealed from her husband.

At length, on some change in public affairs, Mr. Squeeze, who had made an overcharge of some thousand pounds in one article, lost his contract; he was found to owe a large debt to government, and his accounts must be made up immediately. This was impossible; he had not only spent his large income without making any provision for his family, but had contracted heavy debts by gaming and other vices. His creditors poured in upon him. He wrote to Bragwell to borrow another sum, but without hinting at the loss of his contract. These repeated demands made Bragwell so uneasy that, instead of sending him the money, he resolved to go himself secretly to London and judge by his own eyes how things were going on, as his mind strangely misgave him.

He got to Mr. Squeeze's house about eleven at night, and knocked gently, concluding they must be in bed. But what was his astonishment to find the hall was full of men. He pushed through in spite of them, though to his great surprise they insisted on knowing his name. This insulted him; he refused, saying, "I am not ashamed of my name; it will pass for thousands in any market in the west of England. Is this your London manners, not to let a man of my credit in without knowing his name, indeed!"

What was his amazement to see every room as full of card-tables, and of fine gentlemen and ladies, as it would hold; all was so light, and so gay, and so festive, and so grand, that he reproached himself for his suspicions, thought nothing too good for them, and resolved secretly to give Squeeze another five hundred pounds to help to keep up so much grandeur and happiness.

At length seeing a servant he knew, he asked him where were his master and mistress, for he could not pick them out among the company, or rather his ideas were so confused with the splendor of the scene, that he did not know whether they were there or not. The man said that his master had just sent for his lady up stairs, and he believed that he was not well. Mr. Bragwell said he would go up himself and look for his daughter, as he could not speak so freely to her before all that company.

He went up and knocked at the chamber door, and its not being opened made him push it with some violence. He heard a bustling noise within, and again made a fruitless attempt to open the door. At this the noise increased, and Mr. Bragwell was struck to the heart at the sound of a pistol from within. He now kicked so violently against the door that it burst open, when the first sight he saw was his daughter fallen to the ground in a fit, and Mr.

Squeeze dying by a shot from a pistol which was dropping out of his hand.

Mr. Bragwell was not the only person whom the sound of the pistol had alarmed. The servants, the company all heard it, and all ran up to this scene of horror. Those who had the best of the game took care to bring up their tricks in their hands, having had the prudence to leave the very few who could be trusted to watch the stakes, while those who had a prospect of losing, profited by the confusion and threw up their cards. All was dismay and terror. Some ran for a surgeon, others examined the dying man, while some removed Mrs. Squeeze to her bed, while poor Bragwell could neither see, nor hear, nor do anything. One of the company took up a letter that lay open upon the table, addressed to him. They read it, hoping it might explain the horrid mystery. It was as follows:

"To Mr. Bragwell:

"Sir—Fetch home your daughter; I have ruined her, myself, and the child to which she every hour expects to be a mother. I have lost my contract. My debts are immense. You refuse me money; I must die, then; but I will die like a man of spirit. They wait to take me to prison; I would die as I have lived; I invited all this company, and have drunk hard since dinner to get primed for the dreadful deed. My wife refuses to write you for another thousand, and she must take the consequences.

Vanity has been my ruin. It has caused all my crimes. Whoever is resolved to live beyond his income is liable to every sin. He can never say to himself, thus far shalt thou go and no farther. Vanity led me to commit acts of fraud that I might live in splendor; vanity makes me commit self-murder, because I will not live in poverty. The new philosophy says that death is an eternal sleep, but the new philosophy lies. Do you take heed; it is too late for me. The dreadful gulf yawns to swallow—I plunge into perdition. There is no repentance in the grave, no hope in hell.

"Yours,

Dashall Squeeze"

The dead body was removed, and Mr. Bragwell remained almost without speech or motion. The company began to think of retiring, much out-of-humor at having their party so disagreeably broken up; they comforted themselves, however, that as it was so early, for it was now scarcely twelve, they could finish their evening at another party or two—so completely do habits of pleasure, as it is called, harden the heart, and steel it not only against virtuous impressions, but against natural feelings.

Now it was that those who had nightly rioted at the expense of those wretched people were the first to abuse them. Not an offer of assistance was made to this poor forlorn woman, not a word of kindness, or of pity, nothing but censure was now heard. "Why must these upstarts ape people of quality?" though as long as these upstarts could feast them, their vulgarity and their bad character had never been produced against them. "As long as thou doest well unto thyself, men shall speak good of thee."

One guest who, unluckily, had no other house to go to, coolly said, as he walked off, "Squeeze might as well have put off shooting himself till the morning. It was monstrous provoking that he could not wait an hour or two."

As everything in the house was seized, Mr. Bragwell prevailed on his miserable daughter, weak as she was, next morning to set out with him for the country. His acquaintance with polite life was short, but he had seen a great deal in a little time. They had a slow and a sad journey. In about a week, Mrs. Squeeze delivered a dead child, she herself languished a few days and then died, and the afflicted parents saw the two darling objects of their ambition, for whose sakes they had made too much haste to be rich, carried to the land where all things are forgotten.

Mrs. Bragwell's grief, like her other passions, was extravagant; and poor Bragwell's sorrow was rendered so bitter by self-reproach, that he would quite have sunk under it had he not thought of his old expedient in distress, that of sending for Mr. Worthy to comfort him. It was Mr. Worthy's way to warn people of those misfortunes that he saw their faults must bring on them, but not to reproach or desert them when the misfortunes came. He had never been near Bragwell during the short, but flourishing reign of the Squeezes, for he knew that prosperity made the ears deaf, and the heart hard to good counsel; but as soon as he heard his friend was in trouble, he set out to go to him. Bragwell burst out into a violent fit of tears when he saw him, and when he could speak, said, "This trial is more than I can bear."

Mr. Worthy kindly took him by the hand, and when he was a little composed, said, "I will tell you a short story. There was in ancient times a famous man who was a slave. His master, who was very good to him, one day gave him a bitter melon, and bade him eat it; he ate it up without one word of complaint. 'How was it possible,' said the master, 'for you to eat so very nauseous and disagreeable a fruit?' The slave replied, 'My good master, I have received so many favors from your bounty, that it is no wonder if I should once in my life eat one bitter melon from your hands.' This generous answer so struck the master that the history says he gave him his liberty. With such submissive sentiments, my friend, should man receive his portion of sufferings from God, from whom he receives so many blessings. You in particular have received much good at the hand of God; shall you not receive evil, also?"

"O, Mr. Worthy," said Bragwell, "this blow is too heavy for me, I cannot survive this shock; I do not desire it, I only desire to die."

"We are very apt to talk most of dying when we are least fit for it," said Worthy. "This is not the language of that submission which makes us prepare for death, but of that despair which makes us out of humor with life. O, Mr. Bragwell, you are indeed disappointed of the grand ends that made life so delightful to you; but till your heart is humbled, till you are brought to a serious conviction of sin, till you are brought to see what is the true end of life, you can have no hope in death. You think you have no business on earth because those for whose sake you too eagerly heaped up riches are no more. But is there not under the canopy of heaven some afflicted being whom you may yet relieve, some modest merit which you may bring forward, some helpless creature you may save by your advice, some perishing Christian you may sustain by your wealth? When you have no sins of your own to repent of, no mercies of God to be thankful for, no miseries of others to relieve, then, and not till then, I consent you should sink down in despair, and call on death to relieve you."

Mr. Worthy attended his afflicted friend to the funeral of his unhappy daughter and her babe. The solemn service, the committing his late gay and beautiful daughter to darkness, to worms, and to corruption, the sight of the dead infant for whose sake he had resumed all his schemes of vanity and covetousness, when he thought he had got the better of them, the melancholy conviction that all human prosperity ends in "ashes to ashes and dust to dust," had brought down Mr. Bragwell's self-sufficient and haughty soul into something of that humble frame in which Mr. Worthy had wished to see it.

As soon as they returned home, he was beginning to seize the favorable moment for fixing these serious impressions, when they were unseasonably interrupted by the parish officer, who came to ask Mr. Bragwell what he was to do with a poor dying woman who was traveling the country with her child, and was taken in a fit under the churchyard wall. "At first they thought she was dead," said the man, "but finding she still breathed, they have carried her into the workhouse till she could give some account of herself." Mr. Bragwell was impatient at the interruption, which was indeed unseasonable, and told the man he was at that time too much overcome with sorrow to attend to business, but he would give him an answer tomorrow.

"But, my friend," said Mr. Worthy, "the poor woman may die tonight. Your mind is indeed not in a frame for worldly business, but there is no sorrow too great to forbid our attending the calls of duty. An act of Christian charity will not disturb, but improve the seriousness of your spirit; and though you cannot dry your own tears, God may, in great mercy, permit you to dry those of another. This may be one of those occasions for which I told you life was worth keeping. Do let us see this woman."

Bragwell was not in a state either to consent or refuse, and his friend drew him to the workhouse, about the door of which stood a crowd of people.

"She is not dead," said one; "she moves her head."

"But she wants air," said others, while they all, according to custom, pushed so close upon her that it was impossible she could get any. A fine boy of two or three years old stood by her, crying, "Mommy is dead; mommy is starved."

Mr. Worthy went up to the poor woman, holding his friend by the arm. In order to give her air, he untied a large black bonnet which hid her face, when Mr. Bragwell, at that moment casting his eyes on her, saw in this poor stranger the face of his own runaway daughter, Mrs. Incle. He groaned, but could not speak; and as he was turning away to conceal his anguish, the little boy fondly caught hold of his hand, lisping out, "O stay, and give mommy some bread." His heart yearned towards the child; he grasped his little hand in his, while he sorrowfully said to Mr. Worthy, "It is too much; send away the people. It is my dear, naughty child; my punishment is greater than I can bear."

Mr. Worthy desired the people to go and leave the stranger to them, but by this time she was no stranger to any of them. Pale and meager as was her face, and poor and shabby as was her dress, the proud and flaunting Miss Polly Bragwell was easily known by every one present. They went away, but with the mean revenge of little minds, they paid themselves by abuse for all the airs and insolence they had once endured from her. "Pride must have a fall," said one. "I remember when she was too good to speak to a poor body," said another; "Where are her flounces and her finery now? It is come home to her at last. Her child looks as if he would be glad of the worst bit she formerly denied us."

In the meantime Mr. Bragwell had sunk into an old wicker chair that stood behind, and groaned out, "Lord, forgive my hard heart! Lord, subdue my proud heart. 'Create a clean heart, O God, and renew a right spirit within me.'" This was perhaps the first word of genuine prayer he had ever offered up in his whole life. Worthy overheard it, and his heart rejoiced, but this was not a time for talking but doing. He asked Bragwell what was to be done with the unfortunate woman, who now seemed to recover fast, but she did not see them, for they were behind. She embraced her boy, and faintly said, "My child, what shall we do? 'I will arise and go to my father, and say unto him, Father, I have sinned against heaven, and before thee.'"

This was a joyful sound to Mr. Worthy, who began to hope that her heart might be as much changed for the better as her circumstances were altered for the worse; and he valued the goods of fortune so little, and contrition of soul so much, that he began to think the change on the whole might be a happy one. The boy then sprang from his mother and ran to Bragwell, saying, "Do be good to mommy."

Mrs. Incle looking round, now perceived her father; she fell at his feet, saying, "O forgive your guilty child, and save your innocent one from starving." Bragwell sunk down by her, and prayed God to forgive both her and himself, in terms of genuine sorrow. To hear words of real penitence and heartfelt prayers from this once high-minded father and vain daughter was music to Worthy's ears, who thought this moment of outward misery was the only joyful one he had ever spent in the Bragwell family. He was resolved not to interfere, but to let the father's own feelings work out the way in which he was to act.

Bragwell said nothing, but slowly led to his own house, holding the little boy by the hand, and pointing to Worthy to assist the feeble steps of his daughter, who once more entered her father's doors; but the dread of seeing her mother quite overpowered her.

Mrs. Bragwell's heart was not changed, but sorrow had weakened her powers of resistance, and she rather suffered her daughter to come in than gave her a kind reception. She was more astonished than pleased, and, even in this trying moment, was more disgusted with the little boy's mean clothes than delighted with his rosy face. As soon as she had a little recovered, Mr. Bragwell desired his daughter to tell him how she happened to be at that place just at that time.

Part 7

MRS. INCLE'S STORY

In a weak voice she began: "My tale, sir, is short, but mournful. I left your house, dear father, with a heart full of vain triumph. I had no doubt but my husband was a great man, who had put on that disguise to obtain my hand. Judge, then, what I felt to find that he was a needy imposter, who wanted my money, but did not care for me. This discovery, though it mortified, did not humble me. I had neither affection to bear with the man who had deceived me, nor religion to improve by the disappointment. I have found that change of circumstances does not change the heart, till God is pleased to do it. My misfortunes only taught me to rebel more against Him. I thought God unjust. I accused my father. I was envious of my sister. I hated my husband. But never once did I blame myself.

"My husband picked up a wretched subsistence by joining himself to any low scheme of idle pleasure that was going on. He would follow a crook, carry a dice-box, or fiddle at a fair. He was always taunting me for that refinement on which I so much valued myself. 'If I had married a poor working girl,' said he, 'she could now have got her bread, but a fine lady, without money, is a disgrace to herself, a burden to her husband, and a plague to society.' Every trial which affection might have made lighter, we doubled by animosity. At length my husband was detected in using false dice; he fought with his accuser, both were seized by a gang of men, and sent to sea. I was now left to the wide world; and miserable as I had thought myself before, I soon found there were higher degrees of misery. I was near my time, without bread for myself, or hope for my child. I set out on foot in search of the village where I had heard my husband say his friends lived. It was a severe trial to my proud heart to stoop to those low people; but hunger is not delicate, and I was near perishing. My husband's parents received me kindly, saying that though they had nothing but what they earned by their labor, yet I was welcome to share their hard fare, for they trusted that God, who sent mouths, would send meat also. They gave me a small room in their cottage, and furnished me with many necessaries which they denied themselves."

"O, my child," interrupted Bragwell, "every word cuts me to the heart. These poor people gladly gave thee of their little, while thy rich parents left thee to starve."

"How shall I admit," continued Mrs. Incle, "that all this goodness could not soften my heart, for God had not yet touched it. I received all their kindness as a favor done to them. When my father brought me home any little dainty that he could pick up, and my mother kindly dressed it for me, I would not condescend to eat it with them, but devoured it sullenly in my little room alone, suffering them to fetch and carry everything I wanted. As my haughty behavior was not likely to gain their affection, it was plain they did not love me; and as I had no notion that there were any other motives to good actions but fondness, or self-interest, I was puzzled to know what could make them so kind to me, for of the powerful and constraining law of Christian charity I was quite ignorant.

"To cheat the weary hours, I looked about for some books, and found, among a few others of the same kind, 'Doddridge's Rise and Progress of Religion in the Soul.' But all those books were addressed to sinners. Now, as I thought I was not a sinner, I threw them away in disgust. Indeed, they were ill suited to a taste formed by plays and novels, to which reading I chiefly trace my ruin; for, vain as I was, I should never have been guilty of so wild a step as to run away, had not my heart been tainted, and my imagination inflamed, by those pernicious books.

"At length my little George was born. This added to the burden I had brought upon this poor family; but it did not diminish their kindness, and we continued to share their scanty fare without any upbraiding on their part, or any gratitude on mine. Even this poor baby did not soften my heart; I wept over him, indeed, day and night; but they were tears of despair; I was always idle, and wasted those hours in sinful murmurs at his fate, which I should have employed in trying to maintain him. Hardship, grief, and impatience, at length brought on a fever. Death seemed now at hand; and I felt a gloomy satisfaction in the thought of being rid of my miseries, to which, I fear, was added a sullen joy to think that you, sir, and my mother would be plagued to hear of my death when it would be too late; and in this your grief, I anticipated a gloomy sort of revenge.

"But it pleased my merciful God not to let me thus perish in my sins. My poor mother-in-law sent for a good clergyman, who pointed out to me the danger of dying in that hard and unconverted state, so forcibly that I shuddered to find on what a dreadful precipice I stood. He prayed with me, and for me, so earnestly that at length God, who is sometimes pleased to magnify His own glory in awakening those who are dead in trespasses and sins, was pleased, of His free grace, to open my blind eye, and soften my stony heart. I saw myself a sinner, and prayed to be delivered from the wrath of God, in comparison of which the poverty and disgrace I now suffered appeared as nothing.

"To a soul convinced of sin, the news of a Redeemer was a joyful sound. Instead of reproaching Providence, or blaming my parents, or abusing my husband, I now learned to condemn myself, to adore that God who had not cut me off in my ignorance, to pray for pardon for the past and grace for the time to come. I now desired to submit to poverty and hunger in this world, so that I might but live in the fear of God here, and enjoy His favor in the world to come. I now learned to compare my present light sufferings, the consequence of my own sin, with those bitter sufferings of my Saviour that He endured for my sake, and I was ashamed of murmuring. But self-ignorance, conceit, and vanity, were so rooted in me that my progress was very gradual, and I had the sorrow to feel how much the power of long bad habits keeps down the growth of religion in the heart, even after it has begun to take root. I was so ignorant of divine things that I hardly knew words to frame a prayer, but when I got acquainted with the Psalms, I there learned how to pour out the fullness of my heart, while in the gospel I rejoiced to see what great things God had done for my soul.

"I now took down once more from the shelf 'Doddridge's Rise and Progress,' and O with what new eyes did I read it! I now saw clearly that not only the thief and the drunkard, the murderer and the adulterer, are sinners, for that I knew before, but I found that the unbeliever, the selfish, the proud, the worldly-minded—all, in short, who live without God in the world, are sinners. I did not apply the reproofs I met with to my husband, or my father, or other people, as I used to do, but brought them home to myself. In this book I traced, with strong emotions and close self-application, the sinner through his entire course, his first awakening, his convictions, repentance, joys, sorrows, backslidings, and recovery, despondency, and delight, to a triumphant death-bed. And God was pleased to make it a chief instrument in bringing me to myself. Here it is," continued Mrs. Incle, untying her little bundle, and taking out a book, "accept it, my dear father, and I will pray that God may bless it to you as He has done to me.

"When I was able to come down, I passed my time with these good old people, and soon won their affection. I was surprised to find they had very good sense, which I never had thought poor people could have; but indeed, worldly persons do not know how much religion, while it mends the heart, enlightens the understanding also. I now regretted the evenings I had wasted in my solitary room when I might have passed them in reading the Bible with these good folks. This was their refreshment after a weary day, which sweetened the pains of want and age.

"I one day expressed my surprise that my unfortunate husband, the son of such pious parents, should have turned out so ill. The poor old man said, with tears, 'I fear we have been guilty of the sin of Eli; our love was of the wrong sort. Alas, like him, "we honored our son more than God," and God has smitten us for it. We showed him what was right, but through a false indulgence, we did not correct him for what was wrong. We were blind to his faults. He was a handsome boy, with sprightly parts; we took too much delight in those outward things. He soon got above our management, and became vain, idle, and extravagant, and when we sought to restrain him, it was then too late. We humbled ourselves before God; but He was pleased to make our sin become its own punishment. Timothy grew worse and worse till he was forced to flee for a misdemeanor; after which we never saw him, but have heard of his changing from one idle way of life to another, "unstable as water." He has been a servant, a soldier, a shopkeeper, and an actor. With deep sorrow we trace back his vices to our ungoverned fondness; that lively and sharp wit, by which he has been able to carry on such a variety of wild schemes, might, if we had used him to reproof in his youth, have enabled him to do great service for God and his country. But our flattery made him wise in his own conceit, and there is more hope of a fool than of him. We indulged our own vanity, and have destroyed his soul.'"

Here Mr. Worthy stopped Mrs. Incle, saying that whenever he heard it lamented that the children of pious parents often turned out so ill, he could not help thinking there must be frequently something of this sort of error in bringing them up; he knew, indeed, some instances to the contrary, in which the best means have failed; but he believed that, from Eli the priest to Incle the laborer, more than half the failures of this sort might be traced to some mistake, or vanity, or bad judgment, or sinful indulgence in the parents.

"I now looked about," continued Mrs. Incle, "in order to see in what way I could assist my poor mother, regretting more heartily than she did, that I knew no one thing that was of any use. I was so desirous of humbling myself before God and her, that I offered even to try to wash."

"You wash!" exclaimed Bragwell, starting up with great emotion. "Heaven forbid that with such a fortune and education, Miss Bragwell should be seen at a washing-tub."

This vain father, who could bear to hear of her distresses and her sins, could not bear to hear of her washing.

Mr. Worthy stopped him, saying, "As to her fortune, you know you refused to give her any; and as to her education, you see it had not taught her how to do anything better. I am sorry you do not see, in this instance, the beauty of Christian humility. For my own part, I set a greater value on such an active proof of it than on a whole volume of professions."

Mr. Bragwell did not quite understand this, and Mrs. Incle went on.

"What to do to get a penny I knew not. Making ornaments, or fringes, or cutting out paper, or dancing and singing, was of no use in our village. The shopkeeper indeed would have taken me, if I had known anything of accounts; and the clergyman could have got me a nursery-maid's place, if I could have done good work. I made some awkward attempts to learn to spin and knit, when my mother's knitting wheel or knitting lay by, but I spoiled both through my ignorance. At last I luckily thought upon the fine netting I used to make for my trimmings, and it struck me that I might turn this to some little account. I got some twine, and worked early and late to make nets for fishermen, and cabbage-nets. I was so pleased that I had at last found an opportunity to show my good will by this mean work, that I regretted my little George was not big enough to contribute his share to our support by traveling about to sell my nets."

"Cabbage-nets!" exclaimed Mr. Bragwell, "There is no bearing this. Cabbage-nets! My grandson hawk cabbage-nets! How could you think of such a scandalous thing?"

"Sir," said Mrs. Incle mildly, "I am now convinced that nothing is scandalous which is not wicked. Besides, we were in want; and necessity, as well as piety, would have reconciled me to this mean trade." Mr. Bragwell groaned, and bade her go on.

"In the meantime, my little George grew into a fine boy; and I adored the goodness of God, who, in the sweetness of maternal love, had given me a reward for many sufferings. Instead of indulging a gloomy distrust about the fate of this child, I now resigned him to the will of God. Instead of lamenting because he was not likely to be rich, I was resolved to bring him up with such notions as might make him contented to be poor. I thought if I could subdue vanity and selfishness in him, I should make him a happier man than if I had thousands to bestow on him; and I trusted that I should be rewarded for every painful act of present self-denial by the future virtue and happiness of my child.

"Can you believe it, my dear father, my days now passed not unhappily. I worked hard all day, and that alone is a source of happiness beyond what the idle can guess. After my child was asleep at night, I read a chapter in the Bible to my parents, whose eyes now began to fail them. We then thanked God over our frugal supper of potatoes, and talked over the holy men of old, the saints, and the martyrs, who would have thought our homely fare a luxury. We compared our peace, and liberty, and safety, with their bonds, and imprisonment, and tortures, and should have been ashamed of a murmur. We then joined in prayer, in which my absent parents and my husband were never forgotten, and went to rest in charity with the whole world, and at peace in our own souls."

"Oh, my forgiving child" interrupted Mr. Bragwell, sobbing, "and did you really pray for your unnatural father, and did you lie down in rest and peace? Then let me tell you, you were better off than your mother and I were. But no more of this: go on."

"Whether my father-in-law had worked beyond his strength in order to support me and my child, I know not, but he was taken dangerously ill. While he lay in this state, we received an account that my husband was dead in the West Indies of the malaria, which has carried off such numbers of our countrymen. We all wept together, and prayed that his awful death might quicken us in preparing for our own. This shock, joined to the fatigue of nursing her sick husband, soon brought my poor mother to death's door. I nursed them both, and felt a satisfaction in giving them all I had to bestow, my attendance, my tears, and my prayers.

"I, who was once so nice and so proud, so disdainful in the midst of plenty, and so impatient under the smallest inconvenience, was now enabled to glorify God by my activity and my submission. Though the sorrows of my heart were enlarged, I cast my burden on Him who cares for the weary and heavy-laden. After having watched these poor people the whole night, I sat down to breakfast on my dry crust and my coarse dish of tea without a murmur; my greatest grief was lest I should bring away the infection to my dear boy, for the fever had now become putrid. I prayed to know what it was my duty to do between my dying parents and my helpless child. To take care of the sick and aged seemed to be my first duty. So I offered up my child to Him who is the Father of the fatherless, and He spared him to me.

"The cheerful piety with which these good people breathed their last proved to me that the temper of mind with which the pious poor commonly meet death is the grand compensation made them by Providence for all the hardships of their inferior condition. If they have had few joys and comforts in life already, and have still fewer hopes in store, is not all fully made up to them by their being enabled to leave this world with stronger desires of heaven, and without those bitter regrets after the good things of this life which add to the dying tortures of the worldly rich? To the forlorn and destitute, death is not so terrible as it is to him who 'sits at ease in his possessions,' and who fears that this night his soul shall be required of him."

Mr. Bragwell felt this remark more deeply than his daughter meant he should. He wept, and bade her proceed.

"I followed my departed parents to the same grave, and wept over them, but not as one who had no hope. They had neither houses nor lands to leave me, but they left me their Bible, their blessing, and their example, of which I humbly trust I shall feel the benefits when all the riches of this world shall have an end. Their few effects, consisting of some poor household goods, and some working-tools, hardly sufficed to pay their funeral expenses.

"I was soon attacked with the same fever, and saw myself, as I thought, dying the second time; my danger was the same, but my views were changed. I now saw eternity in a more awful light than I had done before, when I wickedly thought death might be gloomily called upon as a refuge from every common trouble. Though I had still reason to be humbled on account of my sin, yet through the grace of God, I saw death stripped of his sting, and robbed of his terrors, 'through Him who loved me, and gave Himself for me,' and in the extremity of pain, 'my soul rejoiced in God my Saviour.'

"I recovered, however, and was chiefly supported by the kind clergyman's charity. When I felt myself nourished and cheered by a little tea or broth, which he daily sent me from his own slender provision, my heart smote me to think how I had daily sat down at home to a plentiful dinner without any sense of thankfulness for my own abundance, and without inquiring whether my poor sick neighbors were starving; and I sorrowfully remembered that what my poor sister and I used to waste through daintiness would now have comfortably fed myself and child. Believe me, my dear mother, a laboring man who has been brought low by a fever might often be restored to his work some weeks sooner if, on his recovery, he was nourished and strengthened by a good bit from a farmer's table. Less than is often thrown to a favorite dog would suffice so that the expense would be almost nothing to the giver, while to the receiver it would bring health and strength and comfort.

"By the time I was tolerably recovered, I was forced to leave the house. I had no human prospect of subsistence. I humbly asked God to direct my steps, and to give me entire obedience to His will. I then cast my eyes mournfully on my child, and though prayer had relieved my heart of a load which without it would have been intolerable, my tears flowed fast while I cried out in the bitterness of my soul, 'How many hired servants of my father's have bread enough and to spare, and I perish with hunger!' This text appeared a kind of answer to my prayer, and gave me courage to make one more attempt to soften you in my favor. I resolved to set out directly to find you, to confess my disobedience, and to beg a scanty pittance with which my child and

I might be meanly supported in some distant country where we should not disgrace our more happy relations. We set out and traveled as fast as my weak health and poor George's little feet and ragged shoes would permit. I brought a little bundle of such work and necessaries as I had left, by selling which we subsisted on the road."

"I hope," interrupted Bragwell, "there were no cabbage-nets in it."

"At least," said her mother, "I hope you did not sell them near home."

"No, I had none left," said Mrs. Incle, "or I should have done it. I got many a lift in a wagon for my child and my bundle, which was a great relief to me. And here I cannot help saying, I wish drivers would not be too hard in their demands if they help a poor sick traveler on a mile or two; it proves a great relief to weary bodies and naked feet, and such little cheap charities may be considered as 'the cup of cold water,' which, if given on right grounds, 'shall not lose its reward.'"

Here, Bragwell sighed, to think that when mounted on his fine bay mare, or driving his neat chaise, it had never once crossed his mind that the poor way-worn foot-traveler was not equally at his ease, or that shoes were a necessary accommodation. Those who want nothing are apt to forget how many there are who want everything.

Mrs. Incle went on: "I got to this village about seven this evening, and while I sat on the churchyard wall to rest and meditate how I should make myself known at home, I saw a funeral. I inquired whose it was, and learned it was my sister's. This was too much for me. I sunk down in a fit, and knew nothing that happened to me from that moment till I found myself in the work-house with my father and Mr. Worthy."

Here Mrs. Incle stopped. Grief, shame, pride, and remorse, had quite overcome Mr. Bragwell. He wept like a child, and said he hoped his daughter would pray for him, for that he was not in a condition to pray for himself, though he found nothing else could give him any comfort. His deep dejection brought on a fit of sickness.

"O," said he, "I now begin to feel an expression in the sacrament which I used to repeat without thinking it had any meaning: 'The remembrance of thy sins is grievous, the burden of them is intolerable.' O, it is awful to think what a sinner a man may be, and yet retain a decent character! How many thousands are in my condition, taking to themselves all the credit of their prosperity, instead of giving God the glory; heaping up riches to their hurt, instead of dealing their bread to the hungry. O let those who hear of the Bragwell family never say that vanity is a little sin. In me, it has been the fruitful parent of a thousand sins—selfishness, hardness of heart, forgetfulness of God. In one of my sons, vanity was the cause of injustice, extravagance, ruin, and self-murder. Both my daughters were undone by vanity, though it only wore the more harmless shape of dress, idleness, and dissipation.

The husband of my daughter Incle it destroyed by leading him to live above his means and to despise labor. Vanity ensnared the souls even of his pious parents, for while it led them to wish to see their son in a better condition, it led them to allow him such indulgences as were unfit for his own.

"O you who hear of this, humble yourselves under the mighty hand of God, resist high thoughts, let every imagination be brought into obedience to the Son of God. If you set a value on finery, look into that grave; behold the moldering body of my Betsy, who now says 'to corruption, Thou art my father; to the worm, Thou art my mother, and my sister.' Look at the bloody and brainless head of her husband. O, Mr. Worthy, how does Providence mock at human foresight? I have been greedy of gain, that the son of Mr. Squeeze might be a great man. He is dead; while the child of Timothy Incle, whom I had doomed to beggary, will be my heir.

"Mr. Worthy, to you I commit this boy's education. Teach him to value his immortal soul more, and the good things of this life less, than I have done. Bring him up in the fear of God, and in the government of his passions. Teach him that unbelief and pride are at the root of all sin. I have found this to my cost. I trusted in my riches; I said, tomorrow shall be as this day, and more abundant. I did not remember, that 'for all these things God would bring me into judgment.' I am not sure that I believed in a judgment. I am not sure that I believed in a God."

Bragwell at length grew better, but he never recovered his spirits. The conduct of Mrs. Incle through life was that of a humble Christian. She sold all her sister's finery, which her father had given her, and gave the money to the poor, saying it did not become one who professed penitence to return to the gaieties of life. Mr. Bragwell did not oppose this; not that he had fully acquired a just notion of the self-denying spirit of religion, but having a head not very clear at making distinctions, he was never able, after the sight of Squeeze's mangled body, to think of gaiety and grandeur without thinking at the same time of a pistol and bloody brains; for, as his first introduction into gay life had presented him with all these objects at one view, he never afterwards could separate them in his mind. He even kept his fine buffet of plate always shut, because it brought to his mind the grand unpaid-for sideboard that he had seen laid out for Mr. Squeeze's supper, to the remembrance of which he could not help taking the idea of debts, prisons, executions, and self-murder.

Mr. Bragwell's heart had been so buried in the love of the world, and evil habits were become so rooted in him, that the progress he made in religion was very slow; yet he earnestly prayed and struggled against vanity, and when his unfeeling wife declared she could not love the boy unless he was called by their name instead of Incle, Mr. Bragwell would never consent, saying, he stood in need of every help against pride. He also got the letter which Squeeze wrote just before he shot himself, framed and glazed;

this he hung up in his chamber, and made it a rule to go and read it as often as he found his heart disposed to vanity.

THE PLOWBOY'S DREAM

I am a plowboy stout and strong
As ever drove a team,
And three years since, asleep in bed,
I had a dreadful dream.

And as that dream has done me good,
I've got it put in rhyme,
That other boys may read and sing
My dream, when they have time.

I thought I drove my master's team,
With Dobbin, Ball, and Star,
Before a stiff and handy plow,
As all my master's are.

But found the ground was baked so hard,
And more like brick than clay,
I could not cut my furrow clean,
Nor would my beasts obey.

The more I whipped, and lashed, and swore,
The less my cattle stirred;
Dobbin lay down, and Ball and Star,
They kicked and snorted hard,

The Plowboy's Dream

When lo, above me, a bright youth
Did seem to hang in air,
With purple wings and golden wand,
As angels painted are,

"Give over, cruel wretch," he cried,
"Nor thus thy beasts abuse;
Think, if the ground was not too hard,
Would they their work refuse?

"Besides, I heard thee curse and swear,
As if dumb beasts could know
What all thy oaths and curses meant,
Or better for them go.

"But though they know not, there is One,
Who knows thy sins full well;
And what shall be thy after-doom,
Another shall thee tell."

No more he said, but light as air,
He vanished from my sight,
And with him went the sun's bright beams
And all was dark midnight.

The thunder roared from under ground
The earth it seemed to gape;
Blue flames broke forth, and in those flames,
A dire gigantic shape.

The Plowboy's Dream

"Soon shall I call thee mine," it cried,
  With voice so dread and deep,
That quivering like an aspen-leaf,
  I wakened from my sleep.

And though I found it but a dream,
  It left upon my mind
That dread of sin, that fear of God,
  Which all should wish to find.

For since that hour, I've never dared
  To use my cattle ill,
And ever feared to curse and swear,
  And hope to do so still.

Now ponder well, ye plowboys all,
  The dream that I have told;
And if it works such change in you,
  'Tis worth its weight in gold;

For should you think it false or true,
  It matters not one pin,
If you but deeds of mercy show,
  And keep your souls from sin.

THE BAD BARGAIN

or

THE WORLD SET UP FOR SALE

By Hannah More

The devil, as the Scriptures show,
Tempts sinful mortals, high and low;
And acting well his various part,
Suits every bribe to every heart;
See, there the prince of darkness stands,
With baits for souls in both his hands.

To one he offers empires whole,
And gives a scepter for a soul!
To one he freely gives in barter
A peerage, or a star and garter;
To one he pays polite attention,
And begs him just to take a pension.

Some are so fired with love of fame,
He bribes them by an empty name;
For fame they toil, they preach, they write;
Give alms, build hospitals, or fight;

The Bad Bargain

For human praise renounce salvation,
And sell their souls for reputation.

But the great gift, the mighty bribe,
Which Satan pours amid the tribe,
Which millions seize with eager haste
And all desire at least to taste,
Is, plodding reader—what do ye think?
Alas, 'tis money, money—chink!

Round the wide world the tempter flies,
Presents to view the glittering prize;
See how he hastes from shore to shore,
And how the nations all adore;
Souls flock by thousands to be sold,
Smit with the foul desire of gold.

See at yon needy tradesman's shop,
The universal tempter stop;
"Wouldst thou," he cries, "increase thy treasures
Use lighter weights and scantier measures;
Thus thou shalt thrive." The trader's willing,
And sells his soul to get a shilling.

Next Satan to a farmer hies;
"I scorn to cheat," the farmer cries;
Yet still his heart on wealth is bent,
And so the devil is content;
Now markets rise, and riches roll,
And Satan quite secures his soul.

The Bad Bargain

Mark next you cheerful youth so jolly,
So fond of laughter and of folly;
He hates a stingy, griping fellow,
But gets each day a little mellow;
To Satan too he sells his soul,
In barter for a flowing bowl.

Thus Satan tries each different state,
With mighty bribes he tempts the great;
The poor with equal force he plies,
But wins them with a humbler prize;
Has gentler arts for young beginners,
And fouler sins for older sinners.

Oft too he cheats our mortal eyes,
For Satan father is of lies;
A thousand swindling tricks he plays us,
And promises but never pays us;
Thus we, poor fools, are strangely caught,
And find we've sold our souls for naught.

Nay, oft, with quite a juggler's art,
He bids the proffered gift depart;
Sets some gay joy before our face,
Then claps a trouble in its place;
Turns up some loss for promised gain,
And conjures pleasure into pain.

Be wise, then, O ye worldly tribe,
Nor sell your conscience for a bribe;

The Bad Bargain

When Satan tempts you to begin,
   Resist him, and refuse to sin;
   Bad is the bargain, on whole,
To gain the world and lose the soul.

THE LADY AND THE PIE

or

KNOW THYSELF

By Hannah More

A worthy squire of sober life,
Had a conceited, boasting wife;
Of him she daily made complaint;
Herself she thought a very saint.
She loved to load mankind with blame,
And on their errors build her fame.
Her favorite subject of dispute
Was Eve, and the forbidden fruit.
"Had I been Eve," she often cried,
"Man had not fallen, nor woman died;
I still had kept the orders given,
Nor for an apple lost my heaven;
To gratify my curious mind,
I never had ruined all mankind;
Nor from a vain desire to know,
Entailed on all my race such woe."
The squire replied, "I fear 'tis true,
The same ill spirit lives in you;

The Lady and the Pie

Tempted alike, I dare believe,
You would have disobeyed, like Eve."
The lady stormed, and still denied
Both curiosity and pride.
The squire, some future day at dinner,
Resolved to try this boastful sinner;
He grieved such vanity possessed her,
And thus in serious terms addressed her:
"Madam, the usual splendid feast,
With which our wedding-day is graced,
With you I must not share today,
For business summons me away.
Of all the dainties I've prepared,
I beg not any may be spared;
Indulge in every costly dish;
Enjoy, 'tis what I really wish;
Only observe one prohibition,
Nor think it a severe condition;
One small dish, which covered stands,
You must not dare to lay your hands.
Go—disobey not, on your life,
Or henceforth you're no more my wife."
The treat was served, the squire was gone,
The murmuring lady dined alone;
She saw whatever could grace a feast,
Or charm the eye, or please the taste;
But while she ranged from this to that,
From venison haunch to turtle fat,
On one small dish she chanced to light,
By a deep cover hid from sight;

The Lady and the Pie

"Oh, here it is—yet not for me!
I must not taste, nay, dare not see.
Why place it there; or why forbid,
That I so much as lift the lid?
Prohibited of this to eat,
I care not for the sumptuous treat.
I wonder if it's fowl or fish;
To know what's there I merely wish.
I'll look—O no, I lose for ever,
If I'm betrayed, my husband's favor.
I own I think it vastly hard,
Nay, tyranny, to be debarred.
John, you may go—the wine's decanted;
I'll ring, or call you, when you're wanted."
Now left alone, she waits no longer,
Temptation presses more and stronger;
"I'll peep—the harm can never be much,
For though I peep, I will not touch;
Why I'm forbid to lift this cover,
One glance will tell, and then 'tis over.
My husband's absent, so is John,
My peeping never can be known."
Trembling, she yielded to her wish,
And raised the cover from the dish;
She starts—for lo, an open pie,
From which six living sparrows fly.
She calls, she screams with wild surprise,
"Haste, John, and catch these birds," she cries;
John hears not, but to crown her shame,
In at her call her husband came.

Sternly he frowned, as thus he spoke:
"Thus is your vowed allegiance broke!
Self-ignorance led you to believe
You did not share the sin of Eve.
Like hers, how blessed was your condition;
Like heaven's, how small my prohibition!
Yet you, though fed with every dainty,
Sat pining in the midst of plenty.
This dish, thus singled from the rest,
Of your obedience was the test;
Your mind, unbroke by self-denial,
Could not sustain this slender trial.
Humility from hence be taught;
Learn candor to another's fault.
Go; know, like Eve, from this sad dinner,
You're both a vain and curious sinner."